Secrets
of
Sandhill Island

by

Peggy Chambers

Secrets of Sandhill Island

Cover Art by *Kim Mendoza*

The Wild Rose Press, Inc.
PO Box 708
Adams Basin, NY 14410-0708
Visit us at www.thewildrosepress.com

Publishing History
First Mainstream Mystery Edition, 2015
Print ISBN 978-1-62830-679-8
Digital ISBN 978-1-62830-680-4

Published in the United States of America

All Evan wanted was to be with Meg.

He would provide for her and the child, or children as the years went by. He was still unsure why she chose him—a fisherman—over anyone else in the world, but she did. Her family didn't like him, but they were just going to have to get used to him.

He struggled pulling the nets in alone. The pulley did most of the work, however it still would have been nice to have some help. The hair on the back of his neck stood up when he sensed the presence behind him. He turned around. The man stood almost close enough to touch. The dark ski mask pulled over his face sent a shiver up Evan's spine. Where did he come from? But, most of all, why did he hide his face out here on the open ocean? And then he saw the giant meat hook in his hand.

"Who are you and how did you get on my boat?" Evan stepped toward the intruder despite the danger. He never expected what came next.

"This is from Graham." The man plunged the hook deep into Evan's chest. Blood spurted every direction as Evan's eyes bulged and he gasped only once. The man in the ski mask quickly pushed him over the side into the dark, churning water.

Dedication

I wish to dedicate this book to my husband, Don, and his encouragement.

Prologue

May, 1983

Evan was used to the waves that rolled his small boat from side to side. He had sea legs, his father would have said. He was so used to the rolling of the boat that he sometimes forgot how to walk on dry land. He leaned over the edge and looked out at the current. The channel always ran southwest this time of year, and moved even faster when a storm approached. The red snapper would be in the channel just waiting to be caught.

Storm clouds gathered in the distance, but he had plenty of time to get his catch in and make it back to the dock before it became too rough. He seldom went out alone, but Rowdy was still down with the flu. Rowdy was getting older and Evan knew the day would come that he should retire. However, Evan doubted that Rowdy would ever retire. He doubted that he could, financially or emotionally. He always said that the sea was his life—and might be his death too.

But, Evan needed to go out today with or without Rowdy. He needed the catch, and the fish were always most active just before a storm. With Meg pregnant, it was time he confronted her father and stood up like a man. The pregnancy wasn't planned. He would have preferred to have a proper wedding and a proper home for both of them before the birth of a child, but nature took another course. Besides, her father was never going to approve of the relationship, but maybe a grandchild for Grandpa Graham might soften the old man. After all, he wasn't in charge of the world, he only thought he was.

All Evan wanted was to be with Meg. He would provide for her and the child, or children as the years went by. He was still unsure why she chose him—a fisherman—over anyone else in the world, but she did. Her family didn't like him, but they were just going to have to get used to him.

He struggled pulling the nets in alone. The pulley did most of the work, however it still would have been nice to have some help. The hair on the back of his neck stood up when he sensed the presence behind him. He turned around. The man stood almost close enough to touch. The dark ski mask pulled over his face sent a shiver up Evan's spine. Where did he come from? But, most of all, why did he hide his face out here on the open ocean? And then he saw the giant meat hook in his hand.

"Who are you and how did you get on my boat?" Evan stepped toward the intruder despite the danger. He never expected what came next.

"This is from Graham." The man plunged the hook deep into Evan's chest. Blood spurted every direction as Evan's eyes bulged and he gasped only once. The man in the ski mask quickly pushed him over the side into the dark, churning water.

****

The body thrown overboard, the man with the meat hook went below to shut off the engine, then reached in and cut the fuel line. Gasoline spewed across the floor. He ran for the exit and quickly climbed back up the steps where the life raft was ready. Just before he stepped in the raft, he threw one lone burning match into the hold. When it met the fuel, it blew and burned brightly. He knew the boat would burn and sink. Any debris would be caught up in the current and head out to sea so nothing would ever be found; just another fisherman who got caught in a storm and never came home. He hoped Graham would think it was worth a bonus that neither the boat nor the body would be found. He started the little engine and headed for home after rinsing the bloody hook in the dark, briny water.

Chapter 1

Present Day

Blue-green waves tumbled over each other in unison foaming up on sugar white sand, leaving tiny crabs and fish behind in the tide pools. The next high tide would carry them back out to the deeper water. In their tiny world, life would go on as it should without the giant ocean reclaiming it. With her skirt tucked up in her waistband, Meg Stanford loved to wade in the tide pools, imagining that she was part of their world some days. But not today. Today she worked in her garden. Her dilapidated beach house sat sentry between the garden and the sea she loved so deeply.

Meg looked up through the lacy shadows of her aging straw garden hat at the sunflowers in front of her. The hat was tattered and torn in places, but still shaded her pale blue eyes from the bright sunlight. She watered her garden again—mostly to wash off the salt that crusted on the plants. She had a series of soaker hoses for the soil. Shore gardening had its own set of problems. Not only was the soil composed mostly of sand—she could add loam to it and improve the texture and nutrients—but there was the relentless wind that blew a wet, salty spray most days. She always said her vegetable stew didn't need to be salted; the tomatoes brought sea salt with them.

South Texas was dotted with islands just slightly off the coast of the mainland. Some inhabited by humans, others only by shorebirds. But, Sandhill Island was a community unto itself. Tourists gathered here, mostly in the summer, and lived the carefree life of beach bums for a few weeks each year. Except for Meg and a few fishermen, the island was only populated in the summer. But, it was her home, winter and summer. She was not a tourist.

Meg picked her garden and placed the produce in the wooden wagon, then pulled them into town to sell each day. Carefully placing the vegetables on the rough wooden planks that served as a table, Meg unfolded the chair she kept behind the shed, hung out the "open" sign and sat down. The Mason jar filled with sunflowers sat in the middle of the table. She hoped someone would need a centerpiece to go with what they bought that day. They mixed well with the sea oats she had gathered. Daylilies, Yarrow, and Lavender would be ready soon. Then, she waited for the first customer of the day. The juicy red tomatoes shone in the sun and the yellow squash curled around each other in a lover's embrace. Green cucumbers completed the still life portrait.

"Mornin', Meg." Mr. Sanders who owned the hardware store across the street waved as he spoke. Always friendly, he never bought her produce. His wife shopped on the mainland and they probably ate vegetables from a can.

"Good morning, Mr. Sanders." She smiled and spoke quietly. If he had a first name, she didn't know what it was.

The tourists began to wander down the street—still

sleepy from the late night in the bars the evening before. They worked all year to get enough money to come down for a week, and then made a living for the locals while they partied.

"Good morning. Are these vegetables fresh or were they picked yesterday?" The man in the khaki shorts and black socks stood in front her with a frown on his face. Maybe he was hung over from last night or maybe he was always grumpy in the morning, it was hard to tell. His face was sunburned and his nose was white with a layer of zinc.

Meg didn't think he would know the difference in fresh picked vegetables. He just wanted to gripe.

"I pick my produce fresh each morning. They're sweetest early in the day."

He picked through the vegetables and pinched the skin of the tomato, bruising it.

"I'll take these." He handed her the two squash and a cucumber. The bruised tomato was left behind. She would probably end up taking it back home with her. Heavy-handed tourists were not her favorite, but she took the good with the bad. She handed his change back and he snorted as if she charged too much.

"Have a good day." He walked away without another word.

Sweat trickled down her neck into the bodice of her faded sundress. The wind was thankfully blowing off the water or it might have been unbearable. She pushed up the patio umbrella on her stand. It was really for the produce not her, but she enjoyed the shade too. Sunscreen was not in her bag of tricks and her aging skin was beginning to show it.

Once the tomatoes left the vine, they didn't fare too

well in the sun so the umbrella helped to keep them fresh. She settled back in her chair, waiting on the tourists to return. The grinding of a key unlocking a door drew her attention and Meg looked up to see a man opening the door to the vacant shop next to her stand.

With his baseball cap down over his eyes, the man carried easels under one arm as he stepped inside. The empty store next door to her lot was opened for the first time since she moved in. The man with a van carried load after load of stretched canvas and boxes of what had to be paint in the front door of the shop. She liked her lot mostly because there were no close neighbors—no one to have to talk to when she didn't feel like talking. But, inevitably, she was going to have to talk now.

He was tall with brownish-gray hair sticking out from under the cap. Sunglasses hid his eyes, but he smiled and nodded when he saw her watching him. She quickly looked away. Soon she heard the hum of the air conditioner—a luxury she didn't have—and the door closed. At least she wouldn't have to keep up a conversation with a perfect stranger. Like most people these days, he would close the doors to keep the cool air in.

The relentless sun beat down and the tourists came back just before dinner. She sold a few more things. Hours passed and most of her vegetables were gone—the sunflowers, however, remained.

"Is there any produce left?" A deep voice from next door roused her from her drowsy state. The man in the baseball cap stood in his doorway, letting the cold air out.

"A few, if you like squash and cucumbers." The bruised tomato lay on its side.

"I'll be right there." He stepped back inside, then quickly reappeared with a worn-out billfold in his hand.

"I'm Alex. I guess we're going to be neighbors. Lucky me, moving in right next to a produce stand—and what beautiful sunflowers. Do you grow all this yourself?" He fondled the bruised tomato.

"Yes, I have a garden with vegetables, herbs, and a few flowers. I'll be here every day. I'm sorry the tomato is squashed. I'll bring more tomorrow."

"It's perfect. I'll take all you have. But a pretty lady like you should have the flowers."

A blush heated her cheeks. "I have plenty of flowers at home. But, you're right, they're lovely in the sunshine."

"Then I'll take the flowers too. I have just the place for them in the shop. I'm an artist and I've rented the shop next door. The landlord is letting me set up a place to sleep in the back, so I'll be here all summer. I guess you live around here?"

"Down on the shore, yes."

Meg gathered the vegetables into a sack and handed them to him, taking the flowers from the Mason jar.

"Um, can I buy the vase too? I don't have anything to put the flowers in."

"Well, I normally bring my flowers in it, but I might have another at home."

"I'll tell you what, you bring me some more flowers tomorrow and we'll trade out the jars."

"You won't need fresh flowers every day. It will start to look like a funeral home."

Alex chuckled. "You're right. Maybe every other day or so, when these die. What did you say your name was?"

"Meg," she said quietly and began to put down the umbrella. The day's sales were done.

"Well, Meg, it was a pleasure to make your acquaintance and I am sure I'll see you tomorrow," he said over his shoulder as he walked away.

"Tomorrow," she mumbled, taking down the sign and folding the chair. Glancing back, she saw her new neighbor place the sunflowers in the window of the shop as she pulled her empty wagon back home.

Chapter 2

The tugboat "The Mosquito" wound its way through the harbor, watching the depth finder for shallow spots. The harbor was changing daily—not nearly as deep as it used to be. Storms and high tides brought more sand all the time. Last week the tug spent days getting the tourist ship off the sandbar. People who didn't know the harbor had no business in it.

The city council tabled the motion for renovation of the harbor at the last meeting. It needed to be dredged again but there just wasn't enough in the coffers. The tugboat captains would make plenty of money this year—at least until the funds were found for dredging. In the meantime, signs were posted to stay on the south side of the harbor to avoid a tow charge.

Mike Fitzgerald was the captain of the little tugboat; a man who made no friends. Friends could be a liability. This year in the shallow harbor, he was going to make sure he had the best chance to make some real money.

Fitzgerald spied Poppy on the dock in the harbor. He had been on this island longer than anyone he knew and he could tell stories about all of the people who lived here. He lived in a shabby apartment in town, but spent most of his time on the dock. Fitzgerald could see him as he guided "The Mosquito" through the harbor. The newcomers—those that weren't born here—could get stranded and that is where "The Mosquito" came in. He could pull them off the sand and to safer water, for a price. Fitzgerald smiled, thinking the bum probably wished he had a tugboat that would make money, too. Fitzgerald was the king of one-upmanship. He liked thinking he was better than most people. But, Poppy didn't have a boat. He just managed to make a living doing odd jobs here and there. There were always hand-outs, and the chef at Le Chez never let anyone starve. He made out okay, for a bum.

From the boat, Fitzgerald saw the woman pulling her wagon back home. Her worn out sundress and sandals lent a Bohemian look to her gray/blonde hair pulled up in a bun. Her brown shoulders and legs made it impossible for a stranger to determine just how old she was. But, she was not a stranger to Fitzgerald. Oh, yes, he knew her. Many people on the island thought she was a newcomer, but he knew better. That broken down beach house she lived in on the shore would have been condemned in a larger city, but Sandhill Island was not a larger city.

He watched her daily, watering her precious garden, toiling from daylight until dark. Something he would never do. She pretended to be a poor woman who lived off the proceeds of a vegetable garden, but he knew better.

Sometimes she would pull her wagon down to the dock to trade vegetables for shrimp with the local fisherman. He never talked to her, but often wondered when she would recognize him.

Then in the evening while he sipped his rum on the boat, he would watch her rocking on her front porch with a glass of iced tea—he was sure she would drink nothing but tea—and dozing until the wind would snap the screen and wake her with a splash of water to her face.

Someday, he would introduce himself again to this woman who had ruined his life. Someday, but not yet. He had a plan simmering in the back of his mind. It had not fully come to fruition, but it was there.

Chapter 3

In her dreams that night, the waves were bigger than a corporate tower. They washed over the tiny boat, soaking her until she couldn't breathe. Gasping, Meg woke up wet, drenched in sweat not sea water, and found she was in her own bed. Outside her window a restless wind blew and lightning crackled in the distance. A storm was brewing, and not just in her dreams. Without warning the rain pelted her tiny bungalow, blowing in on her bed. She rose quickly to shut the windows.

Wrapped in a throw that lay on her couch, she padded outside onto her porch barefoot. The storm clouds gathered around the rising sun. Red sky at morning, sailor take warning, she thought. Her father used to quote that old saying. The wind whipped around and blew a salty spray on everything in its path. It would be impossible to get into the garden for hours even if the storm let up. And she knew she could not sleep in the muggy house with the windows shut.

Instead, she took a shower and put on jeans and a tee shirt, pulled her hair back away from her face in a clip and began cleaning the old house. The tired linoleum floors shone as she scrubbed them with lye soap and a brush in a bucket of water. Most people these days never scrubbed a floor on their hands and knees—but, that was how she was certain the corners contained no grime. She remembered Mariam scrubbing her mother's floors that way.

The rain continued to blow and the wind changed directions over and over. She opened one window and it would rain in and she would have to close it again. She went through the house opening and closing windows as the wind changed its mind about which way to blow. At least she wouldn't have to water the garden today. However, she might not sell a single vegetable. If she couldn't get into the garden to pick them or pull her wagon into town, she would have to stay home.

Finally, the winds let up. But, the rain continued to pound the ground as puddles formed and drops splashed. She might as well rest today, chances were slim she would sell anything. She found a corner near a window and curled up with a book. The rain-cooled air felt good on her warm, moist skin. Soon she was asleep again, but the dream was different this time.

Blue-green water streamed by the side of the boat in the current. It pulled along horizontal to the shore this time of the year and Evan said that was where the fish were. Meg looked out into the distance at dark navy water, so dark it was almost black. The gentle waves rolled up and under the boat and she watched dolphins playing in the distance. Salt air up her nostrils, she breathed it back out slowly. This was home. She loved the sea almost as much as Evan. The deep dark water held secrets it never gave up. She felt his arms around her as she stared out at the water.

Leaning her head back against his chest she felt his lips on her ear and neck. They had been out most of the day and there was sure to be trouble when she got home. Meg feared that her father had guessed she was not with her girlfriends in Corpus Christi for the day as she had said. Rowdy told Evan that Graham had been asking around about him. But, that only pushed her closer to her lover.

His hand slid down the front of her blouse and she arched her back, breathing in his scent deeply. She wanted to stay this way forever; alone on the ocean, miles from anyone or anything, unhurried, and wrapped in his arms.

Pulling her blouse out of her jeans, he slowly unbuttoned it. Her shirt open to the air, she felt the wind caress her body and she turned to wrap her arms around him.

"Come down." He took her hand and led her toward the berth. She looked back at the water one last time as the dolphin splashed next to the boat. Turning back, she found Evan was no longer there. He had gone on without her.

"Evan?" she called, looking down into the interior of the boat where the sleeping quarters and kitchen were. She stepped down the steps, calling his name again.

The boat gently rocked back and forth, and Evan, her beloved fisherman, was nowhere in sight. She searched the boat from one end to the other. Everything was turned upside down. The food in the galley rolled around on the floor, threatening to trip her every step. She called his name over and over, but he never responded. Where was he?

The winds came up and tossed the boat from side to side, slinging her against the closet, knocking her to the ground. A sudden squall blew up while she was looking for her fisherman and she called him again as she climbed the steps. The waves were splashing up over the edge of the boat, whipping her blouse off her shoulders, and she pulled it closed and buttoned it. Where did he go?

Did he fall overboard in the storm? What about her, was she alone on the boat and how would she get home? Scared and unable to find Evan, she berated herself about her concern for her own safety. She couldn't find Evan anywhere and the storm was gathering speed!

She woke with a start and realized she was not on the boat, but again in her own home and the rain had finally stopped.

Wiping the cobwebs from her brain, Meg came back to reality as she walked to the back door to look at the rain-soaked garden. The sandy soil still drained well, even with the addition of the loam she had added over the years. But, even sand had to have time to drain after a deluge. She stared out at the soggy garden.

There in the middle of the squash plants was a fat, brown bunny happily munching her leaves. Leaves she was not willing to share. She sold the best produce to the locals or tourists. The rabbit had no idea how hard it was to grow a garden in a salty environment. She kept only the ugly, twisted, and blemished ones for herself and canned many of them for winter. No, she would not share her vegetables with the rabbit who would take more than his share. How it got to the island she would never know, but he had to go—and she knew she couldn't kill the poor little thing.

Pulling on her rubber boots caked with mud from the last time it rained; she eased the door open slowly and stepped out onto the rickety wooden steps. They leaned to the left even more in the wet soil. Slowly, she went down the steps, eyeing the bunny the entire time. He looked up and munched, his furry nose wiggling. He seemed unconcerned about the giant human looking at him. The squash blossoms and leaves were just too tempting. Meg picked up a piece of a broken clay pot at the bottom of the stairs. She was never a pitcher and she didn't want to hit the rabbit, only scare it.

"Shoo!" She lobbed the shard of pottery at the rabbit. It landed short and the rabbit hardly flinched. Hands on her hips, she looked at her nemeses and he looked back. Picking up a dried branch from beside the house, this time she ran at the furry rodent, yelling and swinging the branch. Grabbing a mouthful of squash blossom with the tiny squash still attached, it turned, hopped to the back of the yard, twisted around, and looked at her once more.

"Go on!" And the rabbit disappeared around the corner and up the sand dune to hide in the grass. But, she knew it would be back. She never had to fence in her garden before, but short of making a rabbit stew, she knew that would be her only means of defense now that the creature had found her little patch of heaven. Besides, her mother always said they were born pregnant—at least, they multiplied like they were. If it came back and brought its whole family, she would be out of business in a week. She walked the length of the garden following the rabbit's footprints and saw all the havoc it had wreaked since the storm finished, shaking her head and wondering what else the furry rodent could do today.

At the back of the yard where the trellises stood she noticed the blackberries were finally ripening.

There might be enough for a basket today. The sun was peeking out from behind the clouds and the squash and tomatoes were ripe and ready to be picked. She was already in the mud and wearing her rubber boots, so she might as well harvest the vegetables.

Grabbing a basket from the back porch, she wandered the rows and picked the freshly washed vegetables. She looked around at her homegrown veggies, some still partially green, and decided to pick everything that was ready, even the ones that were not quite as ripe as she would like, since the rabbit would most likely be back as soon as she was gone. Her wagon would be overflowing on the trip to town today.

Lastly, she picked a pint basket of blackberries. The first berry of the season she kept for herself as she placed it on her tongue and bit down. She did very little for herself in this quiet life she had chosen, but this was one luxury she indulged in. The tart juice filled her mouth with joy, and she smiled, wiping her chin with her sleeve. She knew they would sell first, so she pulled her wagon into the garden and carefully filled it with baskets, leaving the berries for the top.

The wagon overflowing, she tugged and pulled it up the hill into town hoping to sell all that she had. She knew her chances were slim, but if they didn't make it to market, it was a sure bet they would be eaten for free. By the time she got to her stand, she was soaked in sweat from dragging the heavy load.

She stopped at the tiny stand in town and found the tourists were already out and had passed her by. She could hear the air conditioner humming next door.

"Mornin', Meg. Nice rain we got this morning." Mr. Sanders waved as he swept his front porch.

"Yes, very nice."

"You've got a bounty there. I'm surprised you could get into the garden with the mud."

"Boots." She pointed to the muddy rubber boots on her feet. She was still in her jeans and tee shirt with no hat on her head. Unprepared to leave, she pulled her wagon to market without thinking of how she was dressed. It would be a hot day with no hat.

He nodded and smiled as he swept the puddles from around his door.

"You're late. I wondered if you were coming in at all. Nice rain we had this morning." Alex smiled at her from his doorframe, coffee in hand. "The tomato was delicious by the way. Have any more?"

"I'm late because of the wet garden, so I waited until it drained. Yes, I have tomatoes, squash, cucumbers, and blackberries." It all came out sounding stiff. That might have been the longest conversation she had held for months and it didn't come out of her mouth with ease.

The man with the gray-brown hair walked over as she placed her produce on the stand and hung out the open sign. The vegetables filled the little stand to the hilt, and there was still more in the wagon for later. She hoped the tourists came back or she would be carrying much of it back home this evening.

Alex walked along looking at the produce and rearranged it as he went. He picked up several squash and artfully posed them in different positions along the rough wooden stand. When he realized that Meg was watching him, he stopped.

"Sorry, force of habit. I rearrange things to look like I think they should. It used to drive my students crazy when they were painting a still life."

"You're a teacher?"

"Well, used to be. I taught art at the university. Now, I paint what I used to teach. You know what they say, 'those who can, do; those who can't, teach those who do.' Well, I decided to be one of those who do."

"It's wonderful to be able to do what you love in life. The blackberries are the first of the season." She gestured toward the berries.

Alex ran a thumb lightly over the berries and held one up to the light. "Beautiful. I'll take them—and some tomatoes." He began to pick the softer and riper ones, avoiding the ones with a small amount of green.

"What else is growing in your little truck patch?"

"You a vegan?" Meg asked.

"No, just a connoisseur of good food. I know what I like."

"Well, I might not have anything when I get back. There was a rabbit this morning when I walked out back, and he was making himself at home."

"Rabbit huh? Did it get under the fence?"

"I've never fenced the garden in. I hope I don't have to now."

"Well, where there's one rabbit there's normally more. How do you feel about rabbit stew?"

Meg shuddered.

The wrinkles around Alex's eyes deepened, his grin widening. "I'm kidding. Maybe a fence is a better idea."

"I don't know anything about building a fence."

"I'll help. I've built fences for the theater group at school—how much harder can it be?"

"No, I couldn't impose. You have things to do and

that wasn't what I meant when I said I didn't know how. Really. It's okay."

"I insist. We're neighbors and that's what neighbors do—they help each other. You provide me with vegetables and I can help you with the fence. Anyway, if I don't, there might not be any vegetables for me anymore."

"Well, we'll see." The same tourist in the khaki shorts and black socks walked her way with a scowl on his face.

"The cucumber I bought yesterday was bitter. I hope you have a better selection today." He scowled. Flakes of skin were peeling from his red nose.

"I'm sorry. Here, take a free one to make up for it. Try cutting the ends off next time, the center is normally sweeter."

"Humph." He took the cucumber and walked away without buying anything.

"I don't know how you put up with that every day." Alex watched the man walk away with his free cucumber.

"He won't be here very long. Most tourists stay a week or two and then go back home."

"Well, nothing I have eaten from your garden was bitter. Maybe it was just his attitude."

Meg smiled. Her new neighbor was engaging and easy to talk to, unlike most people she encountered.

Alex gathered the produce and placed it in the bag he brought with him. When that bag was full, he pulled another out of his back pocket and began to fill it too.

"You can't eat all that before it ruins," Meg said, eyeing the bags.

"I'll manage." He smiled at her again.

His smile warmed her heart, something that most people didn't do.

"Meg, thank goodness you're here!" Sam, from the restaurant down the street, was trotting toward her with a large basket. "I have an impromptu banquet this evening and don't have enough produce. What do you have? I may have to adjust the menu."

Sam had his regular suppliers and didn't shop at the lowly little produce stand very often.

"The small party of six has turned into twenty-five and maybe more. The back room will be filled with tourists and I need to offer a choice of soup or salad." He browsed the vegetables on the wooden planks. "What about the stuff still in the wagon? Can I look through it?"

"Of course, Sam, come around back and look." She smiled at Alex as she handed him back the change for his purchase. Her giant haul of vegetables might be gone sooner than she thought.

"Okay, how much for the whole kit and caboodle? And can I just borrow the wagon and bring it back?" He had taken everything off the shelf and placed it in his own basket. "Will seventy-five dollars be enough? That's all I have and I'm really in a hurry."

"That's way too much. Here let me weigh the tomatoes."

"No, I don't have time to weigh it all, just take the seventy-five and let me know if I owe you any more." He pulled out a few crisp bills and handed them to her. "Please?"

"Of course. Here, let me help you with that basket while you pull the wagon." She took down the open sign and ran after the chef in her rubber boots as he pulled her wooden wagon to the back door of the restaurant.

Returning to her stand pulling the empty wagon, she saw Alex on his front porch. His porch held several beautiful paintings on display. He sat in a rocker with a glass of iced tea and gestured to the chair next to him. "Take a load off. Now don't say no. You have nothing more to sell. Just sit and have a glass of tea with your new neighbor or you'll make me feel unwanted."

Meg looked at the man she had just met and wondered why she wanted to sit with him. "Okay, but just one glass. I need to get back home to see what kind of damage the little rascal has done to my garden."

"I wanted to talk about that." He poured a glass of tea from the pitcher that sat on the tiny end table between the rockers and handed it to her. "There's plenty of old lumber that I hauled out for the trash when I moved in. We could use it to fence in the garden. We could put my tools and some of the lumber in your wagon and go to work. You don't have anything else to sell today anyway."

"You do." Meg eyed his paintings. The pastel painting was a portrait of a vase of pale pink roses sitting against a blue wall. You could see a window in the background with a placid aqua sea.

"I can do that anytime. That rabbit won't wait."

"These are really beautiful." She walked around the paintings and tried to slow him down. She liked him, but he was being a little pushy for her tastes. Besides, maybe the rabbit moved on to another garden—maybe somewhere in town.

"Thank you. Drink your tea. We have work to do."

"No, really, the rabbit probably went somewhere

else anyway."

"You know that isn't true. To begin with, there aren't any tastier vegetables than yours and if there were, they wouldn't be close. I am sure he is lying in the shade with a full belly right now. So, drink up— we've got a fence to build."

Meg sat in the chair and looked down at the mud caked on her boots. She didn't want it to fall off on his clean porch. But, the truth was she was hot in her jeans and boots and would like to go home and change to something cooler.

"I'll tell you what I'll do. You get that lumber and we'll take it to my house, but if the rabbit is gone, we won't build a fence. I really didn't want a fence anyway. I like the yard to be open."

"Deal. But, he's not gone." Alex smiled knowingly. He got up and began to put the paintings back in the shop. "Grab that pitcher, will you? We'll put it in the frig."

Meg picked up the pitcher and carried it into the shop where the air was cool and inviting. She dared not stay too long or she would never leave. She looked around at his paintings—all in calming pastel colors.

"Lovely colors," she said, surveying the artwork.

"Drab. That's all I have to say on the subject. They sell, but they aren't what I really want to paint."

"What do you want to paint?" she asked.

"The sea and all its brilliant dark shades of blues and greens—sometimes it almost looks black!"

"Yes, I know. It can be very foreboding."

"Okay, bring that wagon of yours around back and we'll pack it up." Alex walked out the back door of the shop.

Hating to leave the cool air, Meg did as she was told and dragged the wagon to the back of the shop where the trash was piled. Alex was digging through the lumber and getting the longest pieces of wood to make a fence. He had no idea how big her garden was and she wasn't going to tell him. He could see for himself.

Chapter 4

After the road ended, Alex pulled the old wagon down the dirt path and over the top of the sand dunes.

Meg pointed. "There, the little house facing the water."

Meg could see the front of her tumble-down house with the screened-in porch. It was tiny with paint peeling, shingles missing, and one dangling shutter. But, it was home. Alex said nothing. Maybe he expected more. As they walked a little further, she could see the beginning of the garden in back. The lovely straight rows and green leaves showed that it was loved and cared for. The back of the house with the rickety steps was a sharp contrast to the perfect garden. It began almost at the back door and went up and stopped at the sloping edge of the sand dunes. The garden was actually bigger than the house in width and length and much better maintained. The rows were straight, with little stone pathways leading to various areas—some for flowers and some for herbs. The vegetables ran down the center. A rabbit's paradise.

Alex cleared his throat. "It's much bigger than I imagined. I don't have nearly enough fencing material."

Meg laughed. "I tried to tell you we couldn't fence it in."

"It's huge! And it's beautiful. You did all this work yourself? How long did it take you?"

"It's still a work in progress. I add soil to it most years and sometimes I put in another addition. I want to try roses, but I don't know how they will handle the salt air."

"A garden on a seashore is tricky, I would think. You have an incredible green thumb." He wandered through the maze of plants, past the lavender and mint, before he reached the tomatoes held up by their vertical cages, and sat on the small wooden bench. It faced the ocean and was shaded by the tall stand of Pampas grass planted behind it. The wind lightly blew the stalks back and forth, making a comforting swishing sound. He looked at the scene with an artist's eye as he surveyed the lovely garden in sharp contrast to the rustic beach house and softly rolling waves of the ocean. He breathed deeply.

"This is heaven. I need to paint this." He walked around in a circle and looking at everything. "Could I...I mean, would it be too much trouble if I set up an easel here sometime? I really need to paint this. The rustic house, the garden, and the sea. That's what I came here for. I wanted to paint the sea."

Meg could see the passion in his eyes as he looked out into the vast blue ocean. She remembered a man with passion in his eyes for the sea once, and she looked away.

"This place is wonderful. I have never seen such beauty and ruggedness in one setting, please say it's okay if I paint it."

Meg cleared her throat. "There are lots of beaches here on the island. Have you checked them out?"

"Not like this. It's the mixture that makes it so inviting. You just don't realize what you've got here. I mean aesthetically. It's perfect to an artist."

"It's home."

"That's it. That's what I'll call the painting. 'It's home.'" The little brown rabbit darted in front of them and dove down the rows toward the okra.

"There he goes!" shouted Alex as he ran after the intruder. Racing around the end of the beans and past the okra, the rabbit outran the man with ease. A giggle rose in Meg's throat as she tried unsuccessfully to stifle it. What would he do with the rabbit if he caught it—like that was going to happen. The harder she tried to contain it, the more the giggle was determined to come out. By the time Alex came back, she had tears streaming down her cheeks and held her stomach.

"Oh, just laugh. I'm an old man and could have had a heart attack chasing that rabbit and my death would be on your hands." He tried to look stern.

"I'm sorry, it was just so funny, the rabbit didn't even break a sweat!" The giggles started again.

Alex stood with his hands on his hips, looking at Meg.

"Okay, okay, I'm sorry. You're right. You came here to help me and all I'm doing is laughing. Would you like to come in for some tea? It's awfully hot out here."

"Tea would be great." He smiled slightly.

Meg led him through the back door and into the tiny, spotless kitchen. "If you want to go through to the porch, I'll bring the drinks." She pointed through the house, toward the ocean.

Meg walked out onto the porch and found Alex in what would have been her front lawn—if she had one. He was standing on the beach looking longingly out to sea.

"I'll say it again. What a view."

"It is lovely. The house needs work, but it suits me fine. I spend most of my time outdoors anyway."

"I think it's great, and I'd like to paint it."

"How will you paint when you are in your studio all the time? You have to sell the paintings you have."

"Well, I'd start by taking some photographs and then, I might close up shop a couple days a week to do the actual easel time. I mean with your permission. I'd promise not to be in the way. Please?"

Meg stared at the man in her front yard and wondered why he was so easy for her to talk to. She normally went out of her way to avoid conversations with most anyone. and yet talking to him was easy. Something about him was trustworthy.

"Okay. You can paint it. I'll be in town anyway selling vegetables."

"Great! And I think I can make a trap for your little bunny friend. I promise not to hurt him. Then maybe we could escort him off the island."

"That would be wonderful. I don't want to kill him, just introduce him to some other buffet than my garden." And she began to laugh again at the thought of the rabbit outrunning Alex.

"You have a great laugh." Alex smiled warmly. "And I need to get back to the shop. How about I bring the camera tomorrow?"

Meg smiled. "That will be fine."

Alex walked back up the hill and Meg watched him go. She found him intriguing in a way that no one had been in a long time. She liked this man.

Chapter 5

The phone woke Meg from a dreamless sleep. It was much too early for phone calls. Jon normally called her on his way to work, but not this early. His days were so busy in Corpus Christi that it was about the only time he had left. And since she was normally up and out the door early too, the timing worked for both of them.

Her only child was an attorney in a large firm in Corpus Christi, miles from his mother and even further from her way of life.

"Did I wake you?" She could tell he was smiling, even through the phone.

"Yes, what time is it?" The sun was barely starting to rise.

"Not quite six yet."

"You go in earlier and earlier. Are you on the road?"

"Yeah, we have a breakfast meeting this morning, so I called a little earlier than normal. I'm sorry to wake you up."

"No problem, I would be getting up soon anyway. You know the garden never sleeps."

"I don't know why you try to kill yourself with that thing. Move back to Corpus Christi. I'll help you get settled in somewhere."

This was not a new conversation. Jon was a good

son and he loved his mother. He worried about her working so hard, especially when she didn't have to. But, most of all, her lifestyle embarrassed him. What if the partners got wind of the fact that his mother was a hermit living on a beach in a tumble-down beach house selling vegetables for a living? He'd be the laughing stock. And then there was Victoria. What would she think of a potential mother-in-law who lived as Meg did?

"I love it here. And yesterday, Sam, the chef at Le Chez, bought all the vegetables I had. Things are looking up!" She neglected to add that it was only because he had an emergency, but she thought it might impress him.

"Okay, whatever makes you happy. Listen, I was hoping I could take you to dinner sometime. I have someone I want you to meet."

"Oh Jon, you know I've given you free reign over the corporation. Philanthropy is big business. The kind of thing an attorney should do, not a gardener."

"You're not a gardener and you know it. You didn't get a master's degree from Wellesley so you could sit on a beach and grow tomatoes."

"They're great tomatoes, and it's not easy growing them on a beach."

"Okay, well think about it. I might be coming to the island soon anyway and I want to see you. Maybe you could make me some of that wonderful gumbo and cornbread."

"Anytime Jon, let me know when you'll be here and I'll get some fresh shrimp."

"Will do. Love you, Mom."

"Love you too, Son. Take care." She clicked the

cell phone off, pushed back the covers, and headed for the shower. She and Jon could not be more different, but they loved each other just the same.

Chapter 6

There he was; her nemesis. Meg saw him when she stepped onto the rickety back step, shading her eyes with one hand. Movement in the cucumbers caught her attention. The little brown rabbit looked up with a mouthful of leaves and stared directly into her eyes. He was much bigger than the last time she had seen him. Was it the same rabbit or his bigger brother? She hoped it was just the same rabbit that had grown immensely from eating her garden, and not a relative. They reproduced so quickly that there could be a dozen of them in a few weeks.

Throwing her hat on her head, she grabbed the rake near the door. Taking a deep breath, she ran at the rabbit, waving the rake in the air with a prehistoric scream. The fuzzy creature dove for cover without even a final bite of food this time.

"Hah! Maybe next time you'll eat grass up on the sand dunes!" But, she knew he wouldn't.

Pulling her wagon to the produce stand, she carefully placed the vegetables on the wooden planks, arranging them in careful groups. Tomatoes, cucumbers, squash, and more blackberries. They were really putting on a show these days. They were fabulous on cereal for breakfast and Meg planned a small cobbler soon. If they kept producing, she might have enough left over for some jam. She remembered

Mariam's jam when she was a child. The hot fresh biscuits dripped homemade butter and wild blackberry jam. They were so warm and flaky they melted in your mouth. But, the jam was the best. It was sweet with just a hint of tartness.

She sat down as Alex walked out of the shop with a camera around his neck and a tripod in his hand. Leaning it against the wall, he locked the door.

"Good morning, Meg." He smiled. "How are the veggies today?"

"Fresh and sweet," she replied, smiling.

"I guess it's still okay for me to take pictures of your place at the beach?"

"Of course. And if you see that ever-fattening little creature, run him out! He was back again this morning."

"I've been working on a trap design that I think will work. We can catch him and keep him in the cage until we can take him off the island. I'll show you when I get back if you're still here."

"I don't know how to thank you Alex. I ran at him like a banshee this morning. If I had neighbors, they would have thought I'd lost my mind."

"I guess your closest neighbors are the fishermen in the harbor."

"Yes, and they're not close, thank heaven. I know I looked like an idiot."

"Meg!" Sam from Le Chez called her from the street. "Please tell me you still have those wonderful blackberries today!"

"You've made a new friend. I'll see you later." Alex turned and left, walking toward the shore.

"Yes, Sam, how many do you want?"

"All you have. And let me look at those wonderful cucumbers! Your produce is so much nicer than anything I can get from my suppliers. I wonder if you would sell to me first before you trade with the tourists. I'd give you top dollar. I could even send someone to pick up if you needed me to."

Meg was surprised. Sam seldom said two words to her until recently when he needed her vegetables, and now he was practically begging for her wares. "Well, if you really want them. They're for sale and you would pay the same price as anyone."

"Wonderful. Maybe I could visit your little garden sometime—and are those lilies? I need centerpieces for this evening. Bring it all! I want everything you have. Here, let me help you pack it back in that wonderful little wagon. My guests will be thrilled. We'll mix the lilies with the sunflowers and sea oats and your fresh vegetables will be the main course tonight. I make a mean Italian vegetable soup. You must try it sometime. It has chicken, rosemary and olives, and now your fresh tomatoes—it is just sublime!"

It was still early in the day, but she had no more vegetables to sell so she would go home to see if the weeds were taking over the tomatoes. Meg pocketed the cash from Sam and began to pull her empty wagon back home in the warm sunshine.

****

At first she thought he was dead. Alex sat on her bench with one arm over the back and his legs crossed in front. The camera—still sitting on the tripod—stood in front of him. His head rolled back and eyes closed, she noticed his chest moving up and down in a rhythmic manner. He was asleep in the shade of the pampas grass.

Placing the handle of the wagon on the ground quietly, she tip-toed around the soundly sleeping man and walked to the back door of her house. She would make the blackberry cobbler and invite him to dinner. She smiled, wondering how long it had been since there had been company in her house. Never, in the house she lived in now. Not since... Well, never.

Turning on the old gas oven, she washed her hands and began making dough for the cobbler as Mariam had taught her. There were just enough berries for a small cobbler, not like the ones that graced her table as a child, but enough for two. Just as she was sprinkling the top crust with sugar to place it in the oven, the door opened and Alex stuck his head in.

"I think I fell asleep," he said. "I saw you through the window. Can I come in? I was waiting for just the right light, and that is the last thing I remember."

"Of course, come in. It's a good thing the rabbit didn't carry you off!" Meg smiled.

"I haven't seen him."

"How could you, your eyes were closed."

"Ah hah! That's probably how he tricked me and got away. Is that a blackberry cobbler?"

"It will be when it comes out of the oven. Would you like to stay for dinner?"

"I couldn't impose. I didn't mean to stay this long. Besides, I have a trap to build."

"Well, there's wood beside the house that we brought here the other day. Will it work?"

"Yes, but I took my tools back home."

The cobbler in the oven, Meg was peeling potatoes into the soup pot. "I was planning a vegetable soup for the entree." She took a covered plastic bowl out of the refrigerator and pulled a large amount of dough from the center, rolling it into a ball and placing it on the round stone pan. "I also have artisan bread and there's cobbler for dessert."

Meg could almost see Alex's mouth water. "I really don't want to be a bother." He stared at the bread dough.

She poured water into the small enamel pan and put it on the burner to simmer as she measured out the loose tea into the water. The scent of freshly brewing tea quickly filled the room as she poured water into the pitcher. Slicing the lemon and placing it on a plate, she put it all on a tray with the tarnished antique silver sugar bowl. She strained the simmered tea into the pitcher, filled two large glasses with ice, and poured the tea over the crackling ice.

"Well, maybe I could stay." He watched her prepare the tea. "I am a little parched."

Meg smiled. "Well, if you really want to." She handed him the glass of tea still warm with melting ice inside. "Here, drink it down, you might need a little more ice. Let's sit out on the porch while this all cooks. It's much cooler out there." And she led him to the front of the house.

After dinner with the dishes done, Alex hung the wet dishtowel on the rack and sighed. "I don't know when I've had anything so delicious."

"Well, thank you. It is mostly that everything is homegrown and fresh. Otherwise it's just vegetable soup. And it was such a pleasure to have someone to eat with. Eating alone is never fun."

"It was wonderful. And that bread—where did you

learn to make that bread?"

"A woman named Mariam taught me to cook. She made that bread recipe often. It's easy and makes a small amount so it's great for a person living alone. I keep it in the refrigerator so I can bake it whenever I need it. By the way, did you get all the shots you wanted today?" Meg put away the last of the dishes as she talked.

"Well, I think I got enough to get started. I know what I want to paint. But, would it be okay if I come back if I need to take more at a later time of day? I mean without falling asleep this time?"

"Whenever you want." Meg smiled at the man in her kitchen who was a stranger just a few days ago.

"I need to go before it gets dark." Alex stood. "Thank you again."

Meg walked him out the back door and through the garden, picking up his camera and tripod. Climbing to the top of the sand dune, she could see a figure in the distance coming her way. His suit coat slung over his shoulder, Jon had parked the Mercedes on the road and was walking the rest of the way. She waved. He stopped and looked at her, waving hesitantly.

"Do you know him?" Alex asked.

"My son." Grinning, Meg ran toward him. "Jon! I thought you were going to call. I didn't get any shrimp."

Meg hugged her only child as he looked over her shoulder at the stranger with the tripod.

"Jon Stanford." Jon held out his hand to Alex. "I'm Meg's son."

"Alex Wallace, Meg's friend."

"And rabbit hunter," Meg giggled. "I have a rabbit

in the garden that Alex is going to help me trap. We just finished dinner, have you eaten? There's plenty left."

"I might be hungry." Jon smiled at his mother.

"Well, I was just on my way back to town. Need to get back to the studio. Meg, thanks again for dinner and the photos. I'll talk to you later. Pleasure to meet you, Jon."

"Likewise," Jon said, warily eyeing the strange man at his mother's house.

Seated at the kitchen table, Jon sipped the tea as he scooped a spoonful of soup. The bread lay buttered on the plate.

"Lord, I miss this." He took a bite of the bread. "You could sell this at some of the fancy restaurants in Corpus Christi for a mint. It's always so wonderful."

"Well, that was what I was telling Alex. It's the fact that it is homemade with love. That's what makes it good. Besides, if I started making it in bulk and marketing it, it wouldn't be nearly as good. It is the small, personal batches that are the best."

"Tell me about Alex. Are you two an item?"

"Jon! Really! I just met him. He is a friend who has a studio next door to me at the produce stand. I was telling him about the rabbit and he is going to help me get rid of the little critter. Then he came out here and fell in love with the view. He is an artist, and he asked if he could paint this place and the sea. He was taking pictures to use for his initial drawings."

"You're a big girl and can take care of yourself, but I just want to be sure you're okay out here all alone. Really, I'm glad you have a friend."

"Evidently, I've got two. Sam at Le Chez in town keeps buying all the produce. He wants to buy almost everything I've got. He says it is much better than what his suppliers have. He came over the other day because he was desperate for veggies with a large crowd coming and then he has been coming back. He even said he would pick up if he needed to. I consider that a compliment."

"Well, like you said, there is nothing like homegrown. You might just be starting up a business. Mariam would be proud."

"Well, I hope so."

"But, I came out here to tell you something and invite you to dinner on the mainland sometime soon." He took a deep breath. "I'm getting married."

"Jon!"

"Her name is Victoria Chung, and I know you will love her as much as I do."

"That's wonderful!"

"Her family is from Corpus Christi and she's a fashion designer. I want you to meet her and take my two leading ladies to dinner sometime soon."

"I'd love to. When do you want to do this?"

"I'll have to check my schedule, but in a couple of weeks, if possible. We are talking about a fall wedding when the weather is a little cooler. Her parents want a big wedding at the country club with the reception outdoors, and in Corpus Christi that needs to be later in the year."

"Country Club. It's been a long time. I may have to go shopping."

"That would be good for you." He stood. "I hate to eat and run, but I have an early meeting in the morning. Promise me you'll take care of yourself and I'll get back with you on the time for dinner."

"I always take care of myself and I'm looking forward to meeting the lovely Victoria." Meg cleared the table and walked Jon out the back door. In the light of the full moon the path was visible through the garden and up the sand dunes to his car. Her thoughts swirled at the latest news—her son was getting married. And then she thought about the last time she was at the country club. She had hoped to never have to go back there again.

Chapter 7

Meg pulled her wagon to the dock where the shrimp boat captain tied his boat. Paul looked up and over the edge of the boat and smiled.

"Veggies!" he shouted to his crew and they all stopped what they were doing.

"Afternoon, Paul. How are the shrimp today?"

"Not as many as yesterday, but still good. What have you got to trade?"

"The cucumbers are taking over as well as the squash. They're both good, but the best thing is the blackberries. I can get you some in the morning. They're all gone today."

"Credit, huh? Do we deal in credit boys?" Paul smiled. "Do they come already baked in a cobbler?"

"They could." Meg returned the smile.

"How many shrimp do you need?"

"Two pounds should be plenty."

"Two pounds it is and that cobbler while it's still warm."

"Deal. How about some lilies for that lovely wife of yours?"

"My lovely wife? My lovely wife ran off last month with some guy from Corpus Christi—and good riddance!"

Meg's mouth dropped open and she stammered. "Paul, I'm sorry, I didn't know. Please forgive me."

A grin began at the corners of his mouth and then spread into a hardy laugh. "I couldn't run that woman off if I tried. She loves shrimp too much!" He laughed even harder at his own joke.

"Oh Paul, you're terrible. Here, take the poor woman some flowers. After all, she has to put up with you." She gave him the lilies as the bag of shrimp was handed over the side of the boat.

"You gentlemen have a good evening." Meg walked away down the dock she had known all her life.

The old man they called Poppy lounged in the chair that might, or might not, have belonged to him. Sometimes he had a fishing pole and caught his dinner. Today he was sitting in the late afternoon sun smiling with the fishing pole in the water. Whether or not he caught something was anyone's guess.

Meg stopped the wagon in front of him and smiled. Poppy was a fixture on Sandhill Island. He had been around as long as anyone could remember. No one knew how old he was or how he arrived at the island. He had just always been there. He watched the world go by, but never got involved.

Meg knew he ran errands for her dad sometimes when she was a child and Graham paid him cash— probably not much—but at least he was paid for his trouble. She picked a few vegetables and handed them to the fisherman. "To go with your catch." She smiled as she walked away.

"Thankee," he said, never looking up.

Walking past, she saw the man leaning against the boathouse with his hat pushed down over his eyes. He tried not to look at her. He was there most days when she came down to the dock. He always made her nervous the way he stood around, but never talked to anyone. She thought he owned a tugboat, but when he wasn't working he just stood around on the dock and watched the people come and go.

"Nice veggies you got there, ma'am."

Meg looked back, startled. He spoke to her.

"Thank you. Would you like some?"

"No thanks, just making a comment." He looked at her from under the hat. "I see you all the time and you never speak."

"Well, you've never spoken to me either." What was with this guy?

"You don't remember me, do you?" He pushed the hat back. His vaguely familiar eyes bored into her.

She stared at him. "Should I?"

"Mike Fitzgerald." He gazed intently at her. "I was Rowdy's son. You remember Rowdy, Evan's fishing partner?"

Meg jumped just hearing Evan's name. It had been such a long time. And no one on the island knew about her past. She immediately looked around to see if anyone was listening.

"You must have me mistaken for someone else." She quickly began to walk away once more.

"I'm not mistaken. I know who you are." He grabbed her arm.

"What do you want?" She pulled away, rubbing the place where he'd gripped her.

"I don't want anything. I just thought you should know that someone around here has guessed who the hermit lady with the vegetable patch really is. I mean, what are you hiding from? I see that kid of yours in his shiny Mercedes coming to visit his momma now and then. It took a while, but then I remembered he was raised in Corpus Christi by his mom and probably still lived there."

"I don't know what you're talking about. I have to go." She raced down the dock.

Once on the beach, she ran as fast as the wagon would pull through the sand. Back in her garden, she dropped the handle at the back door and ran in, slamming the back door and leaning against it. She didn't empty the wagon. The rabbit could have the produce.

How could this happen? She thought she could get away from her past, from her family, and just live out her life doing what she loved best. She didn't need to be a Stanford anymore. Those days were gone. If it weren't for Jon, she would have left Corpus Christi and never looked back. But, he was her life. He was at least the good part of her life. He belonged to her and Evan. He was all that was left of his father.

Her cell phone rang. The screen said simply "Jon."

"Hello, Jon." She took a deep breath to try and make her voice sound normal.

"Hey, Mom. You okay?"

"Yes, why?"

"Well, you just sounded a little rattled. Your rabbit's not back is it?"

"Well, I haven't seen it, but you never know."

He chuckled. "Well, I called because I'd like for you to come to Corpus this weekend and meet Victoria. I can have the car pick you up at the ferry and you can spend the day, and then it can take you back later. You could even spend the night with me and go back the next day."

"Oh, Jon. I didn't realize it would be so soon. I haven't got a thing to wear and my hair is a mess. I'm just not prepared."

"Well, let's get you prepared. You take the early ferry and I'll have Joan make an appointment for you at your old stylist for the works. And then shopping. That way you'll be ready for dinner that evening. You can spend the whole day. It would be good for you. Then like I said, you can spend the night with me and go back on the ferry the next morning."

Meg thought about her old life. Her old stylist. What would he think of her now with her stringy hair and skin unprotected from the elements? Did she want to go back to that? She knew they would make fun of her behind her back. She wished she had a friend to talk to about all of it. But, that was what she left behind in Corpus Christi. Friends that weren't so friendly anymore.

"Mom? Are you still there?" Jon asked.

"I'm here, I was just thinking."

"Well, you want to meet her, don't you?"

"Of course!" Meg said. "Of course I want to meet her, it is just so soon and so unexpected."

"It's just a little shopping and dinner. You can do it."

"Yes, of course you're right." Meg stood a little taller and thought about her son. She would do anything for him—she always would, and he felt the same about her. Of course she could—would—do this. "I'll take the eight o'clock ferry."

"Great. Greg will be waiting with the car."

"Okay, see you Saturday." She clicked off the phone without even saying I love you and felt apprehensive about the day to come. What was she thinking going back to Corpus Christi?

Chapter 8

The eight-by-ten photos of Meg's property tacked on the rough paneled wall; Alex picked up the brush and stared at the canvas. He would start with the sea. After all, that was what he came here to paint—the ocean in all its colors and moods. Placid blue to angry black, it was all beautiful to Alex. The sea had a personality like a person. One day it was up and the next day it was down, depending upon internal and external factors.

He painted for hours, standing in his studio that doubled as a sales room. No customers came in or wanted to see the paintings that were displayed in his window. Just as well. He didn't want to be disturbed today, even though he could use the money.

The grant he secured was to take care of him for a year. But, it was going to be a short year with the price of materials and rent. He was frugal, but he still had to eat.

As a professor, he helped his students find funding all the time and had access to grants for starving artists, but never applied for one himself. Then after the fiasco at the university, Alex felt it was time for a change. He called it the Chauncey Factor. The change in his academic life that caused the change in his personal life.

She was a beautiful young woman—no one would

disagree with that. She had everything in life she could ever want or need. That kind of wealth could make a spirit poor. She had never wanted for anything and was not used to being turned down. When she decided what she wanted was an older professor for a plaything, she expected that it would be given freely as usual. Alex surprised her. He knew her father was on the board of regents for the university—people talk. And he was careful in her grading. His boss had mentioned that at the beginning of the semester. Don't upset the apple cart, he had said. But, as it turned out, he didn't need to grade her carefully. She was a talented artist. Talented, beautiful, and spoiled.

She often found reasons to stay after class when he needed to prepare for the next one. Then she began showing up at his office after hours as he was trying to shut down after a long day. His office hours were posted on the door, and he made sure his students retained a copy at the beginning of each semester. But, she came late anyway—after everyone left.

At first she wanted to talk about art, the kind she painted. Then she delved into art in general to get him into the discussion. He tried to tell her kindly that he needed to go, but she pretended not to hear. Then the day came. The storm blew in as forecast. Evening was going to come much earlier than normal that fall day. He closed the blinds and picked up his briefcase when the door opened without a knock.

"Professor Wallace," she said as she came in the door. She was dressed in heels and a straight skirt with a silk blouse tucked in. Alex looked her over. She didn't look like the traditional student in jeans and a tee shirt. She looked much older, and he was certain that was the plan.

"Chauncey, I was just leaving. You'll need to come back at another time. Maybe make an appointment next time. Besides, the storm outside is getting worse." He didn't know the storm inside was just beginning.

"No, I think I'll stay." She unbuttoned her blouse as she walked toward him, revealing a pink lace bra. Somehow he imagined it would be black. She took the briefcase from his hand and placed it carefully on the desk. Then reaching up, she began loosening his tie.

Alex felt he was watching from afar. He had heard of other professors in this same predicament, but it had never happened to him. He knew the rules about fraternizing with students. He was a single man and he knew that made him even more vulnerable. He reached for the knot in the tie and stepped back, but she held on to his hand and placed it on her breast.

"Chauncey!" Alex said, jerking his hand back. "We can't do this. I'm your teacher and there are rules."

"Rules are made to be broken." She laughed and leaned in to kiss him.

"Not with me. It could mean my job and I'm not going down that road."

"You can find another job."

Alex laughed. "You have no idea what finding a job is all about. You've never worked a day in your life and probably never will." He was surprised how easily it came out of his mouth. His supervisor's words rang in his ears. Don't upset the apple cart. He knew he could be in trouble.

"Don't you want me, Professor?" she crooned.

"That's not the point, Chauncey. You have to leave." He opened the door to usher her out, but she stood her ground.

"No," was all she said.

"Please, it's for the best."

"Really? For whom?"

"For both of us."

"I really don't see the problem—two consenting adults..."

"I'm not consenting. Now go." He tried to sound stern.

She looked him in the eye, her hand running down the front of her open blouse. She stared at him a moment longer and then huffed. Not used to being refused, she turned and stormed out the door. That was the last he saw of her until the campus police knocked on his door the next day, followed by the local police detective. She was charging him with attempted rape. They had photos of her torn blouse. She had run away in the storm to the police station and shown up wet and bedraggled with a story ready for the papers. He would pay for his treatment of her.

****

Alex stared at the painting as he rolled Meg's blackberry back and forth between his fingers and then squashed it in frustration. The colors weren't right, it was too artificial looking. He grabbed the canvas and tossed it across the room. Sweat trickled down his neck and he ran his hands through his hair.

"Well, that was a little childish," he said out loud. The frustration welling up inside him like a tumor, he decided maybe he had painted for the masses too long instead of himself. It looked like a sofa painting at a starving artist show. You couldn't feel the intensity of the sea—it looked like a pastel still-life—the kind that

57

made him a meager living. Rubbing his eyes, he walked to the tiny kitchen for a drink and caught his reflection in the mirror above the sink. Blackberry juice smeared across his eye made him look like he had been in a bar fight. His thumb and forefinger were covered with the black/blue berry juice and it was smeared across the canvas that was thrown across the room as well. He walked to the canvas that lay on the floor, and there on the corner of what was to be a painting, was a smear of the color he had been looking for. The dark blue color of the sea that was in nature, not his paints. It was in the berry. He could never mix that color the way he wanted it, only nature itself could do that.

What if he used the berries for the color of the sea? And the other vegetables that were in his kitchen, like the tomatoes, might be useable too. He would give the pigment a good sealing afterward, but maybe it was the idea he had been looking for. Organic paints made from nature might be his new medium. He grabbed a fresh canvas, crushed the berries into a container as he wiped off his brush, and began to paint again. The berry stain was more the consistency of watercolor. And the effect was mesmerizing.

Chapter 9

Wrapped in a towel, Meg went through her closet again looking for something to wear to the city. Most of her clothes were sundresses and jeans—things to wear in the garden. But, today was different. She scrubbed and shaved in the tub that morning, trying to make her tanned skin look presentable. The lotion in the bathroom was cheap and did little to alleviate the dried out body she seldom noticed.

There in the back of the closet was the yellow linen sheath still hanging in the dry cleaner's bag, unworn since the day she moved in. She had no idea if sheaths were still in style, but it had matching flats, and it would be cool and comfortable. In the back of the bottom drawer of her dresser was the box with the "nice underwear," also unworn for years. Expensive silk panties were an extravagance she no longer needed, until today.

She looked in the mirror at the old woman she had become; splotchy, wrinkled skin, stringy hair beginning to gray, and she sighed. You could run away from your past, but you couldn't run away from your age. What would Max and the others think of her? Would they giggle behind her back or just feel sorry for her? She didn't need their sympathy. She had made her choices happily and lived her life these last few years for herself. If she wanted to atone for the sins of her family by giving their money to people and things that needed it, that was her business. She didn't need the money herself. She saw to it that her son was taken care of and the rest could be given away. So why now was she feeling ashamed of what she had become?

She would not endure their pity or their questions. She would hold her head up high and be the good mother she had always been. She would do what she must for her son and his happiness. He was getting married and she would present herself to the bride in the best manner she knew. She would do it for him, but not for the others that wanted to make fun of her choices in life.

Slipping the yellow dress over her head and zipping it, she realized it was looser than the last time it was worn. She had probably lost weight working in the garden. She sat at the vanity and brushed her stringy blond hair away from her face. Opening the jewelry box, she found the silver clip that Mariam had given her when she was young. She pulled her hair up in a twist, clipping it high on her head, then rubbed a little lip gloss on her wrinkled lips. There, she looked presentable. She turned and looked at herself from the back. Almost.

Reaching for the scarf and purse that matched the dress, she walked to the back door. There was knocking. No one ever knocked on her door and she froze in place. Thinking of the man with the hat over his eyes on the dock, she peeked around the corner where she could see. Alex stood with his back to her looking out into the garden. She let her breath out slowly—she was being silly thinking of Fitzgerald, it was just Alex.

She was unsure at first about having to explain her outfit—she was obviously leaving the house—but, knew he would understand. After all, she could make a day trip if she wanted, couldn't she?

"Alex," she said, opening the door. "How nice to see you."

He stared at Meg in her yellow dress, then slowly spoke. "You look lovely, Meg. Going somewhere?"

"Yes, to the mainland to visit my son. If you want to paint today, please make yourself at home. There's a pitcher of tea in the refrigerator. I have to go and meet the ferry." She eased out the door.

"Well, let me run get the van and you won't have to walk all that way."

"All that way? This whole island isn't a mile wide, how far could it be?" She laughed.

"Well, at least let me walk you. I've something I wanted to discuss with you anyway. Would that be okay? I mean I won't slow you down." He set down the easel and paints next to the broken down back steps.

"Okay, if you would like. I'd enjoy the company."

"I want to say again how lovely you look."

"Thank you Alex."

"And I'm not trying to pry, but you seem all dressed up for something special."

"Jon announced the other night that he is to be married and wants me to meet his fiancée. We're having dinner tonight, but first I'm going to get my hair done. It's been a while."

"Well you can't walk around alone in Corpus Christi—I'll go get the van and drive you."

"He is sending someone to pick me up." She almost said 'sending the car to pick me up,' but

61

'sending someone to pick me up' sounded less stuffy.

"Oh, okay, I just didn't want you stranded, I mean..."

"Alex, I've been to Corpus Christi before and know my way around. I'll be fine. Now what did you want to talk to me about?"

"Oh, well I was distracted by how beautiful you look today."

Meg smiled.

"But, I wondered if it was okay if I picked a few veggies today? I won't take many and I'd be happy to pay for them. I just need a few."

"Of course, take what you need. And you can pay me by watering tonight, if you don't mind. I don't know when I'll be home. The soaker hoses are hooked up, just turn on the faucet for about an hour and then back off—I mean after you have finished your painting of course. I don't want you to get anything wet."

"Of course, I'd be happy to. But, if you know what time you will be back, I could meet you at the ferry."

"I really don't know. I may spend the night with my son so it would be a great help to me if you would do the watering. Then I won't have to worry."

The ferry maneuvered toward the dock, easily slipping into position. The tug boat pilot made the trip from the island to the mainland and back again four times a day except holidays. It was like threading a needle, the way he negotiated the waves and the dock. And he never missed. After the cars drove off and the few going back pulled into position, the pedestrians walked across the plank and found a seat. Meg sat at the back as far away from the spray as she could get so to not get her linen dress wet. No one looked at her strangely. They probably thought she was a tourist returning from a visit, not the crazy veggie lady from the island.

The long black limo shined in the sun at the ferry dock. Greg stood beside the back door ready to open it the moment she arrived. He looked a little older than the last time she saw him, but still possessed the same rugged good looks in his uniform. How he managed to always look cool in the suit standing in the sun, she would never understand.

"Ms. Stanford, it has been too long." He smiled and opened the door for her. The refrigerated air puffed out and engulfed her.

"Greg, handsome as ever, it is always a pleasure. How are the wife and kids?"

"Wife is fine and the kids are growing like weeds. The oldest starts college in the fall."

"Oh, that can't be! I remember that he used to love to ride up front with you when he was just a little tyke! College!"

"And his sister will right behind him in a couple of years."

The drive through town looked much the same as the last time she was here. She watched the ships leaving the harbor and the traffic on the freeways. She was glad she didn't have to live here every day.

At the curb, Greg opened the door to the spa for her. The smells brought home thoughts and feelings she had long forgotten. Max stood by the door in white linen pants and a silk shirt with a geometric print. He looked right past her at Greg and then back to Meg again, startled.

"Ms. Stanford! How nice to see you!" He had a

nasally, high-pitched voice, the one he used to feign surprise. "Honey, how long has it been?" He took her purse and led her to the back. "Jon says to give you the works, and that is exactly what we're gonna do. Star is in place for your body scrub and massage, then Matilda will make your toes and fingers sparkle, while Annie gives you a facial you won't soon forget! We'll finish it off with a new do for your hair—honey what have you done to your hair, that clip has just got to go!" he said, loosening her hair around her shoulders.

"Let me have the clip, it's an heirloom..."

"I'll just put it in your purse." He looked down his nose at Mariam's gift. "But first, let me get you a mimosa. Claire makes the most wonderful mimosas. You're just going to love it!"

Meg soon found herself seated in the thick terrycloth robe, sipping a mimosa. And Max was right about one thing, Claire could make a mimosa to die for.

Scrubbed, rubbed and oiled, Meg emerged from the spa in her robe again and was led out to the salon. Claire stood ready with a bottle of water and another mimosa. Evidently, her only job was to get the client drunk. And it was working. Meg couldn't remember when she felt so deliciously relaxed and pampered. Everything was done for her. A polish in a deep shade of rose was chosen for her nails—she might have chosen a pale pink—and then she found out why.

"Girl, you are gonna' love what Claire did while you were being kneaded and scrubbed." Max turned her chair around so she could see.

The lovely Claire had replaced her beverage tray with hangers holding two outfits that just happened to be in Meg's size.

"They came from your favorite little boutique. And by the way, they said you need to come see them more often."

The first hanger held a pale green Capri set in silk with just a touch of stretch. The buttons on the jacket that doubled as a blouse were a deep pink that almost matched her nail polish. In the bag with them was a beautiful pair of sandals in the same green and pink colors to show off the new pedicure.

But, on the second hanger was a gorgeous iridescent chiffon dress that looked pink and coral at the same time depending upon the light. The sleeveless dress had a silver belt at the lightly gathered waist and a v-neckline. The sling-back pumps were in a bone color with a peep toe so you could see a splash of color from her toes. A deep rose bag matched both outfits.

"Jon said to make his mother look spectacular and you know that we always do what we are told. Well, almost always!" Max winked as he chuckled. "So, what do you think? The dress for dinner tonight?"

"Max, you are amazing! I haven't seen anything this pretty in—well, maybe never." Meg reached for the chiffon.

"Oh no you don't! That manicure isn't dry yet. Keep the fingers still. We'll do the work! And speaking of work, what are we going to do with this mop of hair you've been growing since I don't know when? I'm thinking maybe some highlights around the face and then a cut that doesn't scream 1970. Maybe some layers to give it a kick. You just leave everything to me." He turned her around in the chair to face the mirror.

"Okay, but don't go overboard, Max. I still want to look like me."

"You'll look like you, honey, only better—at least ten years younger. By the way girl, where HAVE you been?"

Max chattered on into the afternoon as he colored and cut Meg's hair. He talked about his business, and everyone else's. Meg told him she lived on the island now, but didn't mention that she was a recluse living off the proceeds of a garden in her backyard. The less he knew, the better.

When her hair was dry, Annie applied Meg's makeup. She reminded her not to get it too thick. Meg wanted to still look like herself. Just a touch of coral lipstick set it off beautifully.

Max still curled and uncurled her now chin-length hair, making it straight and then curly until he finally found just the right combination, then surrounded her with a fog of hairspray.

Meg hardly recognized herself in the mirror—but Max was right, she looked ten years younger. She was ushered into the dressing room where her new clothes hung, and with her nails dry was left to at least dress herself.

"I couldn't believe it was her at first!" The voice that was probably Claire's spoke outside the dressing room. "She looked so old!"

"I heard she was a recluse these days," Max said. "With all that money, why would she go into hiding unless she was trying to hide something? I mean if the money was mine, I'd party, girl!"

"I was told that when she had Jon her family was really upset. Thirty years ago that was a big deal. They never did find the boyfriend's body. Rumor was that her family had him killed. But really, how old is she?

She looks a hundred with that sun damaged skin!"

"I know. Did you see that hair? I mean a girl needs a little primping now and then, even a recluse! All our hard work will probably just go out the window as soon as she gets home. I don't understand, girl."

Meg listened to the conversation through the paper-thin walls, her face burning. This was just what she was afraid of when she left home. Why did she agree to this? She was better off at her beach house. The relaxed feeling she had was shattered. She hadn't felt like this since the last time she was in Corpus Christi. But, she had two choices. She could sit here and listen to this or she could get up and confront the people talking about her. In her new Capri outfit with the yellow dress in a bag, she reached for the door with her deep pink fingertips and walked out.

"Don't you look pretty!" Max stared at her outfit up and down.

"Thank you Max." Meg held her head high. "Thank you for all you've done. But, you know what? I looked pretty when I walked in here. A person's worth is not only skin deep you know."

"Of course! I didn't mean that."

"I don't appreciate you talking behind my back. Did you think I couldn't hear you? That was shallow of you. The way I choose to spend my life and the reasons why are my own, not yours." Max and his employee stood wide-eyed not knowing what to say.

"Is my ride here? Please get my bags." Meg looked from Max back to Claire.

"I think so Ms. Stanford," Max said quietly. "And I'm so sorry that you heard that. I meant no harm and shouldn't have said anything. We just love you that's all, and want the best for you. Please forgive us." He walked her to the front door where Greg was standing. Max handed Greg the clothes.

"Hon, do us both a favor and use this, and come back soon." Max gave Meg a large and expensive tube of sunscreen and a peck on the cheek.

But Meg wondered if she would ever go back.

Chapter 10

Meg arrived at the restaurant and gave her name to the maître'd. Jon sat in the corner of the dim room; a hurricane lamp on his table kept the darkness at bay. He sat close to a woman, his blond hair in deep contrast to her dark features. The stunning young woman's long black hair shone in the candlelight as she smiled at her companion. They seemed comfortable together. Meg was certain this was not a first date.

"My two favorite women at the same table." Jon pulled the chair out for his mother as she walked up, then leaned across to gesture to the woman still sitting.

"Mom, I want you to meet my fiancée, Victoria Chung. My mother, Meg Stanford."

Victoria stood and grasped Meg's hand, her almond eyes sparkling. "So pleased to meet you Meg. Jon talks about his mother all the time. And what a lovely dress."

"Thank you. It's a pleasure to meet the woman who makes my son so happy." Meg looked the slender woman over. She wore a simple cream colored sheath with black pearls at the neckline. Obviously sheaths were still in style.

Jon filled his mother's wine glass and ordered another bottle. The couple had been here a while and almost drained the first.

"I took the liberty of ordering for you," Jon said.

"Swordfish and steamed vegetables and be sure to save room for dessert. The cheesecake is wonderful."

The conversation was pleasant and Meg felt comfortable with her new daughter-in-law to be when the food arrived. Victoria was from a shipping family in the Corpus Christi area. Meg was certain she had heard her father speak of the Chung family before but she wasn't sure why.

Jon was right about the cheesecake—and the wine. He was wonderful at choosing dinner, and it was certain he knew his way around Corpus Christi society; a thing that Meg never quite got the hang of. The conversation light with the wine flowing, Meg began to yawn after the second glass and Victoria took the cue.

"I'm sorry to have to break up this party, but I really have to go. I have an early appointment." Victoria laid her napkin aside and rose.

"I am so glad to meet you," Meg said as she too stood. "I hope that we can spend more time together and get better acquainted. I would love to meet your family sometime also."

"I'm sure they look forward to meeting you too." Victoria kissed Jon and walked toward the exit.

"Well, it's late and you've missed the last ferry. You can spend the night with me and I'll have Greg take you to the ferry in the morning." Jon signed the credit card receipt and took Meg's arm. They left the restaurant together.

In Jon's apartment overlooking the Corpus Christi skyline, he gestured to the couch for her to sit. Spread on the coffee table were court documents. She tried not to look, they were probably confidential. After all, Jon lived alone and didn't have to worry about someone reading his work.

But, the name Alexander C. Wallace jumped out from the heading on the pleading. Alex Wallace, her new friend in town.

"Jon, what is this? Have you been checking up on Alex?"

"Your new beau has a record, Mom." Jon picked up the papers and handed them to her.

"Alex is a friend, not a beau, and why did you look him up?"

"Because you're my mother and I want to look after you. The charge is sexual misconduct with a student. Not a nice thing for a professor, do you think?"

Meg picked up the paperwork and looked it over. "She wasn't under-age," she said after reading the highlights.

"No, but there are rules about teachers and students. The documents were sealed by her father so they wouldn't be public knowledge. I'm sure the family didn't want the embarrassment of the case hanging over their heads."

"So how did you get them?"

"I have a friend who owed me a favor." Jon grinned slyly. A grin Meg had seen many times on her father. She didn't always like the way he was changing as he grew up. He would always be her son, but he had some Stanford in him—like his grandfather.

"Well, this was impertinent of you! I didn't ask you to check up on Alex. He is an artist who moved in next to the vegetable stand and he is helping with the problems in the garden. He even watered for me tonight while I was away."

"I know you don't think I should check up on you,

but you need to realize that people will take advantage of you if you don't watch them. I don't like the fact that a sexual predator is moving in on my mother!"

"He was acquitted." Meg gestured at the documents. "Besides, how do we know what happened? She obviously dropped the charges, and then her father had the case sealed. Doesn't that tell you something? She wasn't under-age, so why did they do it?"

"Like I said, her father was protecting her—just like I am trying to do for you."

"Or she had something to hide."

"Oh good grief! Mom, listen to me. That guy is bad news and you would do well to stay away from him, I'll get you another place for the vegetable stand."

"I don't want another place, and I want you to get out of my personal business."

"You are my personal business. We're family and family looks after one another. You taught me that."

"Well, maybe I taught you too much. Jon, I appreciate what you are trying to do, but I think I'm old enough to pick my own friends!"

Meg looked up at Jon as she sat on the couch in the chiffon dress someone else selected for her. She knew how he felt about her lifestyle and whether or not she was capable of choosing her own friends—just like her father. She hid from the world instead of meeting it head on like he did. He shook his head.

"Okay." He tossed the documents on the coffee table. "I'm going to bed. Greg will be available to take you back to the ferry when you're ready tomorrow. You know where the guest bedroom is." He stomped off to his bedroom and slammed the door behind him.

Chapter 11

Alex leaned the painting against the wall in the tiny kitchen. It was a splash of color in an otherwise drab room. He painted from memory, but the detail was not what was important, it was the subject. Then he walked back outside to his easel in the garden.

He hadn't seen the rabbit in the last few days. He probably did his dining early in the day.

Squeezing the tomato on the pallet, he picked the seeds out. He needed a small sifter or something to strain the seeds. Maybe a tea strainer, he thought, eyeing the back door of Meg's house. No, he couldn't start helping himself to her things. But a tea strainer would be perfect. Every time he painted with the vegetables, he found another hurdle to clear. But the medium was worth it. He had finally found the colors that his eye saw in the ocean.

He painted faster and faster as the muse pushed him forward. He was finally able to paint what his soul saw, not just his eyes. The sea in all its glory. He wanted to paint it at every angle, and every time of day. He longed to paint in a storm, even though he knew that wasn't possible, unless Meg would let him move inside. But, he had probably already intruded enough. He hoped the gift he left on her table would help pay for the time he spent in her garden.

She wasn't like most women. She knew her own

mind and didn't want anything from him. She was self-sufficient, even if she hid from the world. It was obvious that her son had money—at least, he drove a Mercedes and wore a suit to work. So, why did he let his mother struggle with living the way she did and not help her out? Did she refuse him?

He wanted to get to know her better, but after the last disaster he was wary of relationships with women. Not that Chauncey was a relationship, but one way or another it ended in disaster. He never had time in his life for romance. His art was his romance, but yet as he aged, there was a hole in his life—a hole that he didn't know how to fill. And it lingered.

He would ask Meg to dinner—a real date. He wasn't sure she would accept, but he could try. After all, he should pay her back for the opportunity her home had given him. The scenery, the location, and now the new painting medium were exactly what he needed all these years even though he hadn't known it.

He wondered how she would feel if she knew why he was hiding from the world. After he lost his job at the university, he decided to try to paint for a living. The grant he applied for the year before was available, so he took it. It was a good opportunity at the time, and now it was marvelous. He had almost forgotten that Chauncey had cost him his job and his reputation. Almost. But, starting over might have been just what he needed.

He stood back and looked at his masterpiece. Cleaning his brushes, he decided to quit for the day—the light he wanted was gone and he should be, too, by the time she returned. He still had a garden to water.

Chapter 12

Meg arrived at her island the next morning in the yellow sheath with a bag in her hand. Inside were the two new outfits and the court papers Jon gave her. She hadn't slept well the night before and was glad to be home and back in her routine.

Opening the creaky door, she entered her kitchen. Everything was in order in this house that she had always loved. But, her eye was drawn to the one new item in the kitchen. A painting on the kitchen table leaned against the wall. It was bright and cheerful—a woman in a yellow dress and familiar straw hat stood with her back to the portrait, picking berries. The colors were vibrant and alive, and underneath the bright green leaves in the corner was the quivering nose of a rabbit poking out and looking hesitantly up at the intruder in his garden. It was clear who had left the art on her table.

Meg eyed the picture with her hand raised to her mouth. She almost cried. It was beautiful, and it cheered up her drab kitchen. She stood staring at the painting from every angle and smiled. She would hang it on the wall so the sunshine would catch it every morning.

Changing into gardening clothes, she pulled the soon-full vegetable wagon into town, placing the worn out hat on her head as she went.

"Morning Meg. How was dinner and the new

addition to the family?" Alex stood in his doorway, coffee cup in hand.

"Hello Alex." She placed the vegetables on the wooden planks of her stand. "Dinner was fine." A sudden gust of wind blew the hat from her head. Reaching around to capture it, she twisted back toward Alex.

"You cut your hair! It looks lovely. And a manicure too! Very nice."

"Thank you. I said I was getting my hair done before dinner yesterday. By the way, the painting was beautiful. It goes so well in the kitchen. I'm going to hang it tonight, right over the table where it gets the morning light. The colors are so delightful."

"You're welcome."

"But, where's the sea? I thought you were going to paint the sea."

"I am. And I have a new medium for that. Come, let me show you. I want you to be the first. After all, you were the inspiration."

He led her through the shop to the back. Sitting on the easel was an unfinished painting of the ocean at its most magnificent. The waves tumbled to the shore and curled back into the sea in a dark angry color with only the very tips of the wave in a pale green. The sky was still unfinished, but you could see that a storm was coming. Meg knew that sea. It was the one she dreamed about when she dreamed of Evan. The navy and green water rolled, re-exciting itself with every twist.

"Alex, this is wonderful. I've never seen such emotion in colors. What's new about the medium?"

"That's what I wanted to show you. You should be the first to see this because you helped create it." He reached into the refrigerator and pulled out the bowl of blackberries and raspberries. He pinched one and held it out to her. She watched the color drip off his thumb.

"I don't understand," she said, questioning.

"Neither did I at first. It was an accident when I smeared it across the canvas and it stained."

"This is painted with berries?"

"Your berries and other produce. Organic art—that is what I'm going to call it. I don't know if the salt air affects it, but the colors stay brilliant. When I'm finished, I'll seal it well in case it decides to fade. It's an experiment. I don't normally paint with watercolors, but this is about that consistency and it has been fun learning to work with the different feel of the paint."

Meg looked up at the shadow coming through the window. She had a customer. "It's great, Alex, I want to see more. But, I've got to wait on this customer. I'll talk to you later." She walked back to her produce stand to see what the tourist needed, when she heard footsteps from down the street.

"Meg!" Sam from Le Chez was almost running again. It seemed that the only time he ran was when he needed something. Lately what he needed were her veggies.

"Thank goodness you're here. I need it all—again! The truck didn't make it in on time and well, can you bring them to the back door of the restaurant?"

"Of course, Sam. Maybe we need to make a schedule and that would be better for both of us."

"A schedule! You have never managed a restaurant have you?" The sweat ran down his face.

Meg loaded up her wagon again as another customer came by looking over the cucumbers.

"Help yourself. I am packing up. But, take what you want first."

"You're getting fairly popular." Alex stood in the doorway with a glass in his hand. Meg smiled. "Stop in for iced tea on your way back."

Empty wagon trailing behind her, Meg walked back to the produce stand. Her days had changed lately. She didn't spend nearly as much time trying to sell the produce after she grew it, and she'd made some new friends. Life was funny, just when you tried to block it out, it always found a way back in.

Alex sat on his porch with the ice tea pitcher on the table between two rocking chairs. Meg wondered if the town was starting to talk about them. And then she wondered if she cared. She liked talking to Alex, and it was nice to be known by her name again instead of the crazy hermit lady with the produce stand. She knew she would never want to integrate herself back into Corpus Christi society, but she was beginning to enjoy her neighbors here on the island. Alex and his paintings, Sam, the chef at Le Chez, Paul the shrimper and his silly teasing attitude about his wife, and then a shiver went down her spine when she thought of Mike Fitzgerald, the man on the dock who hid behind his hat and tried to scare her. Could he really be Rowdy's son, and did he know something about Evan's death, after all these years? Why was she so afraid of him and what did he want of her? She made a mental note to look through the locker under her bed. The one with her father's papers and the few things she had left of Evan's. Maybe it would shed some light on the Fitzgeralds, Rowdy and Mike.

"You know, I was thinking," began Alex as he

gestured to the chair beside him. "Maybe we should find out what Sam is doing with all those vegetables. I mean, can he cook? Have you ever eaten at Le Chez?"

Meg shook her head.

"Well, what do you say we do that? Want to have dinner sometime and see if the chef is as good as the produce he buys?"

A smile began to light up Meg's face. Was Alex asking her for a date? It had been a long time since she had been asked on a date—but he was probably just being nice. "I've never been there. I normally do my own cooking."

"Well, it's time then. Someone should look after you for a little bit. I know you ate out in Corpus Christi the other night. What was on the menu?"

"Jon ordered for me before I got there, and we had swordfish, steamed veggies, and lots of wine. At least they did. I think they had quite a bit before I got there. I guess she might have been nervous about meeting the future mother-in-law."

"Well, that's just silly. I'm sure she was in love with you before the evening was over."

"She seemed like a nice person. Very attractive and intelligent—very much Jon's equal. I am sure I've heard her family name before. She is a fashion designer, but her family was in shipping years ago."

"Was your family in shipping?"

Meg was aware she had said too much. Alex was so easy to talk to she sometimes forgot herself. She really didn't want to share with him, or anyone else on the island, about her family. That was why she came here—to get away. "I really don't like to talk about my family. Jon is all I have left. He is my family now."

"Of course, I didn't mean to pry, I was just making conversation. But, you're going to have another in your family soon and who knows little ones too, eventually."

"I have no idea if they want children. I didn't ask."

"Well, about Le Chez, how about dinner some night?"

"Is this like a date or are you just feeling sorry for me?"

"Sorry for you? For what? I've never felt anything except admiration for you, living and doing what you want. And I have never seen anything like that garden! No, I am not sorry for you or about meeting you. Yes, I am asking you on a date, unless that makes you nervous, and then it is just two friends having dinner."

Meg stared at the man who had been a stranger just a few days ago. "I would like to have dinner with you Alex, but it would have to be just friendly. I haven't dated in a long time and I'm out of practice."

"That's okay, neither have I. It seems I've spent most of my life wrapped up in my teaching career and now my painting. So, maybe it's time I branched out and included people in my little corner of the world. I like you, Meg, and I would like to see more of you, if that's okay. If I make your nervous, just say so. Like I said, I'm out of practice too."

Meg smiled at the man in front of her. He made her feel relaxed and welcome in a world that she didn't always understand. "Here is my cell phone number. That way you can call me when you want to make a reservation, I mean if Le Chez takes reservations."

He took out his cell phone and placed her in his contacts. "And here's mine so we can keep in touch."

Chapter 13

Meg pulled the locker from under the bed. The photo albums on top she laid aside. She resisted the urge to look at Jon's baby pictures until later. First, she wanted to look through her father's records.

An old fashioned double entry bookkeeping journal in her lap, she slid her legs out from under her and sat on the creaky wooden floorboards. Turning the pages, she ran her finger down the names of customers. She found it, "Chung Shipping." She was right. There was a Chung in her father's list of business associates and something about it rang a bad bell. Conversations around the dinner table that she was not allowed to enter into as a child, nor did she want to, still hung like moldy cobwebs in her mind. But, she was sure her father's face would turn red when he mentioned the name. Chung must have been a competitor.

She never knew why she kept the boxes of receipts and invoices from the days he worked on the dock. His office sat next to the shrimp boats that came and went. She loved spending time with him at work. Even if he was a hard man. He ruled over those who worked for him with an iron fist, as well as her mother, but he was always gentle with Meg. He called her his princess. A sign of the time, she wasn't allowed to speak to the customers or workers. She was a child. But, she watched intently as he wheeled and dealed his way through life. He was a shrewd businessman and he planned after she graduated from college that she would take over his business someday. That day never came.

Meg grew up on Sandhill Island with her parents, but her mother insisted she go to private school on the mainland. Many days when Meg and her mother took the ferry to Corpus Christi for school, her mother would spend the day in the city with her friends until she was forced to go back to the tiny island and its inhabitants when Meg was finished with classes. Alice Stanford longed to go back to Corpus and the life she lived as a young woman before marrying Graham and being forced to live on the island where he worked.

In the summers at her father's office, Meg often wandered down the shore to the tiny beach house that Mariam was allowed to rent from her family. Mariam cooked the meals and scrubbed the floors for Meg's mother. She had been the family maid even before Meg was born. She raised a small garden in her mother's backyard for the family's consumption and was allowed a few things if there were too many to eat. But, most of the extras were canned for the Stanford's winter months.

Meg remembered her soft gray eyes and hair to match pulled back in a bun as she hummed to herself working up a sweat. She always had a kind word for everyone—even Meg's father—and Meg thought of her as more of a maternal figure than her own mother. She taught her to cook and garden until Alice Stanford would come and take her daughter back inside to clean up for some meeting or party in Corpus that Meg was obligated to attend.

During the summer on days that Meg went to work

with her father, she would often be found napping in the hammock that hung on the screened porch of Mariam's rented bungalow. She was a child and could only listen to so many business deals before becoming bored. But, she never tired of listening to the waves roll up on the shore in front of the sleepy little beach house where Mariam lived.

Later, home after graduation from Wellesley, Meg and her father argued most every evening. His princess had grown up. She studied Sociology, not business as he had planned. She decided that shipping was not what she wanted to do with her life, and Corpus Christi society was not for her, either. She planned to look for a job somewhere away from Corpus Christi—or maybe pursue her doctorate, but life got in the way.

That was the summer that she met Evan. She kept him a secret at first. He was a fisherman who docked his boat every evening near her father's office. Her mother wanted her to meet and marry someone from Corpus Christi's society elite. Her father wanted her to take over his shipping business when he retired. She wanted neither of those things.

Saying she was going out with friends, she would steal away and meet Evan at some predetermined place and then they would often sneak back on to his boat after her father left his office. Already in love with the ocean, she would fall in love with the fisherman who earned his living—however meager—from it. Soon, young love turned to passion on his boat tied up at the harbor, and consequently Jon was conceived.

Even though the sexual revolution had taken place at least ten years earlier, Meg's parents and the society they belonged to did not take kindly to a young woman pregnant without benefit of a marriage certificate. Meg was told by the old family doctor the day she swallowed her pride and made an appointment that the birth control pills would not protect her immediately, but she didn't listen. She was certain of only one thing—her love for Evan. Her father was certain his daughter would not become the wife of a fisherman with a leaky boat.

In the stack of invoices, Meg found one with Chung Shipping written on the top of the document. It was for dredging the harbor. Meg remembered that her father was not a fan of dredging. He said if the ocean had plans for where its sand should go, then mankind should respect its authority. If the truth were known, Graham Stanford had other ideas in mind, like tugboats making more money in the years that the sand was deposited into the harbor. He had purchased a couple of tugs years earlier to tow his ships in and out of the harbor, but like many other things in his life, he didn't let them sit idle. If they could make money doing other things, then put them to work. Looking through the ledger, she could find no entry for the payment of the dredging charge.

Another invoice just said "Poppy." She wondered what the old man really did for her father. Not that he was old then, but Meg always thought of him as ancient.

A knock on the door brought Meg back to the present. Walking to the kitchen, she could see Alex leaning to the left as he stood on her crooked back steps. She needed to hire someone to fix them and maybe a few other things around the house. She would talk to the man that owned the hardware store and see if he could recommend a contractor.

"Come in." Meg opened the back door and found Alex standing with a wooden box in one hand.

"I brought my version of a critter trap." He smiled. In his left hand was a box with wire screen on the side for windows and wire on the bottom. There was a door that opened at one end. It barely looked large enough for the rabbit the last time she saw him.

"Do you think it's big enough? He's growing every time I see him." Meg stepped out onto the steps to investigate the box.

"Then we'd better bait the trap and get the little creature out of here. Have you seen him lately?"

"No, we've been missing each other. I guess that is to his advantage. He probably has a watch and knows what time I leave in the morning."

"Like the hare in *Alice in Wonderland*?"

Meg giggled at the thought of her rabbit in a coat and pocket watch serving tea. "I guess. How does this work?"

"Well, we place it in the last place you saw him, and then bait it with something you know he loves. He should just walk in and the door will shut behind him. It won't hurt him, and we can keep him fed and watered until we can escort him off the island."

Meg led Alex with the trap in hand up to the bare ground where squash used to grow. The last place she'd seen the rabbit feeding. He placed the box on the ground and threaded a squash leaf and blossom through the wire floor of the trap. Then propped the door open. When the rabbit went inside, the door would close behind him and he could munch happily on the squash until someone came along and found him. Meg retrieved a jar lid for water and placed it next to the threaded squash so the poor bunny could have a drink after he made a meal of the squash he loved so much.

"Thirsty work. How about some tea?"

"Sure," Alex replied, and they walked back to the house for refreshment. Meg never thought about how much iced tea she drank in the summer months until she met Alex. It was a southern thing; you always had tea to offer your guests. Now it seemed she was always going to the store for more.

Pouring two large glasses from the pitcher in the refrigerator, Meg carried them into the living room. "Do you want to sit on the front porch?" She asked the question without looking up at Alex. He was standing by her coffee table, court documents in hand, glaring at her.

"Where did you get these? Are you checking up on me? These were sealed documents. How did you get them? Did Jon have someone unseal them?"

"Alex." Meg forgot about the documents that were lying on the table. Why hadn't she put them back in the envelope? She never intended to talk to Alex about the situation unless he brought it up first. She hoped it was all just a big misunderstanding that he would tell her about some day. But, this was bound to ruin her only friendship in years.

Alex threw the papers back on the table and stomped off through the house toward the back door. "I would have told you about that, Meg. Jon didn't need to check up on me for his Momma. Or did you ask him to?"

"No! I never asked him to check up on you. And he shouldn't have. I should have gotten rid of the documents. I never should have looked at them at all. I'm sorry, please forgive me." But, it was too late. Alex was out the door and up the path, never hearing the words that came from her heart.

Chapter 14

Meg sat for a while sipping her tea and scanning the documents after Alex left. What was she thinking, leaving them out in the open? It was like she wanted him to see them. Of course she hadn't, but any psychologist might have said otherwise.

She placed the documents back in the envelope, laid them on the coffee table, then walked out the door to the garden. She could just barely see the trap. The noise she heard earlier could have been anything. But maybe it was the trap being sprung.

Walking up the hill carefully, she peeked between the leaves of the tomatoes. There looking out the screen windows of the contraption was a fuzzy, wiggly nose with two brown eyes and long brown ears. Her nemesis was trapped—and he barely noticed. He was too intent on munching on the thing that got him into this predicament to begin with. The tiny squash that he loved was still attached to the vine and pulled through the screen on the bottom of the trap so he could reach it. Life was good.

Alex had attached a handle on the top of the cage so she could carry it. But, with the rabbit inside it was much too heavy to make it all the way to the ferry by hand. On her knees, she peeked in the trap—the bunny looked back without a care. With her hands underneath the box, she dug the squash up and then shoved it, roots and all, into the bottom of the trap with the rabbit. Then she went for her wagon. She could pull the wagon with the trap sitting inside it and take the rabbit to the mainland on the ferry. She didn't like leaving him in the trap any longer than was necessary in the heat of the day. The sooner the rabbit left her island, the better off they both would be.

At the water's edge she caused heads to turn as she pulled the rickety wagon onto the ferry. The crazy veggie lady was back. And what did she have in the wagon this time? Meg was used to their stares, but this time it seemed a little more than ridiculous. Anyone close enough to see into the cage would know she had a rabbit and probably wondered if she was selling them too these days. Most people just looked away when they saw her glance back at them.

The waves were getting larger as the wind increased and she had to hold on to the cage the whole ride to keep it from falling. The weather appeared more unstable the last few days as the threat of storms came and went. Anyone who lived near the ocean knew it was getting close to hurricane season.

After the bumpy ride on the ferry to the mainland was over and the ferry docked, Meg pulled the wagon down the beach away from the hustle and bustle of cars and tourists to a place that was quiet, so that she could release the creature. Setting the trap down on the ground, she opened the door. The bunny just looked at her, munching away on what was left of the leaf and roots.

Why wasn't he scared? Why did he not quickly bolt to get away from the human that had entrapped him? Maybe because his belly was so full he couldn't run.

"Go on, shoo!" Meg said to the lazy rabbit, tapping the side of the cage. He continued to stare at her as he munched comfortably. "Shoo!" she shouted, more loudly and people from the ferry looked up.

Finally, she picked up one end of the trap and dumped him onto the ground. He hopped once and turned to look at her with big brown eyes. She quickly put the trap back on the wagon and barely made it back to the ferry before it began its return trip to the island.

Once onboard the ferry, she stared at the empty cage, realizing he was gone. A feeling tugged at her heart strings. How could she miss the little vermin who was eating her garden? But, she knew even if he was destroying her way of life, she enjoyed his company. She was tired of being alone. The rabbit showed her that she needed to share her life, even if it was only with a fuzzy creature that was unwelcome in her garden.

Tomorrow she would talk to Alex and try to make amends—convince him she didn't mean to pry. It was beginning to dawn on her that she needed to be around people again and Alex was the one she most wanted to spend her time with.

Surely Alex couldn't stay mad at her, could he?

Chapter 15

Mike Fitzgerald wound his tugboat through the harbor, staying away from the ever increasing sand bars. He'd made more money this summer than any he could ever remember. Boats were constantly stuck and having to call for help. However, if this kept up, the shrimpers would leave for another harbor that they could use. There wasn't enough money to fix the sandy mess and that was fine with Mike, at least for now. But, he was afraid the end was in sight. His time on the island could be running out.

Pulling up and tying off, he spotted Meg dragging her wagon back home. She was later than usual. It was almost dark and she never stayed out that late. The tourists were already in the bars and not out buying veggies. Something large and wooden sat in the middle of the wagon as she pulled it back to the broken-down beach house she lived in.

Maybe it was time to pay her a visit and see just what she knew about the death of her lover. He had been trying to find just the right excuse to talk to her lately. After all, it concerned him too. After Evan failed to return the day of the storm, Rowdy was unemployed. He was too old to get a job with another fisherman, and it wasn't like he was capable of doing anything else. He soon fell into a drunken depression and never recovered. Mike's mother had died a few years earlier and it was just the two of them.

Many nights Mike had to get his dad out of the bar in town and bring him home. There wasn't enough money for food and booze, so often Mike went to bed without dinner because his father drank up what little money he was able to make after Evan's death. Mike was forced to raise himself without parents and consequently blamed the Stanfords for his misfortunes. If the young society girl hadn't found herself a beau from the wrong side of the tracks, maybe Mike would have had a normal home life. It was her fault that Evan had to die. Rumor had it that Graham Stanford had him killed as soon as he found out she was pregnant, and Mike knew who did it.

The island was a small town then, much as it was now. There weren't that many players in the game. The other shipper had it in for old man Stanford anyway, the way Mike heard it, especially after Graham hired Chung's ner'-do-well nephew for the job to kill Evan. Chung was lucky to keep the kid on the right side of the law most of the time, and a little bit of money was all it took to get him to go the other way.

Meg had money and Mike thought he deserved a little of it for keeping his mouth shut all these years about the secrets of Sandhill Island and the Stanfords. The people around here didn't seem to know who Meg was or who the daddy of that bastard kid of hers was. But he did, and maybe it was time she paid for his silence.

He watched from a distance as she unloaded the wagon and walked up the rickety steps in the back door of her house. Following her between the huge garden and the house, he wondered what he would do if she refused to pay. The garden could be trashed with little work. It would serve her right after she ruined his life. But, first he would give her a chance to pay up.

He opened the backdoor without noise and stepped onto the back porch where the garden tools and boots sat.

Chapter 16

Her head involuntarily jerked back toward movement in the kitchen as Meg walked to her bathroom. She realized she was not alone in the house. Her heart beat faster and the hair on her neck prickled as adrenaline coursed through her veins. Jumping back from the shadow, she saw a man with a hat. She backed up behind the door facing as sweat ran down the front of her blouse.

"Come out, come out, wherever you are," he said in a sing-song voice. "I seeeeeee you."

Her first instinct was to run, but the house was so small catching her would be too easy. He stood between her and the back door and could grab her on the way out the front. She knew it was the man from the dock with the hat down low that had spoken to her the other day. He said he was Rowdy Fitzgerald's son—the son of her lover's fishing partner. She remembered meeting Rowdy once, but knew nothing about him.

"What do you want?" Her voice trembled. That was probably the first thing anyone said when they were confronted with danger. He rounded the corner and stood in front of her.

"I want to talk to you. You ran away too quickly the other day."

"Talk about what?"

"About you, and Evan, and my dad. Did you know

that Rowdy had a son? Did you, Miss High Society?"

"I only met your dad once and no, I didn't know he had children. But, what has that got to do with me?"

"Exactly the response I expected. You didn't know and you didn't care."

"I don't see how Rowdy's son has anything to do with me. Evan died in a storm and left me a single mother." She eased toward the front door as she talked. Maybe she would try to make a run for it after all. She couldn't see any weapons on the man, but he had broken into her house after dark and was threatening her. That was enough reason to be scared.

She needed to get the lock fixed on the back door like Jon told her. She was sure he was being paranoid when she ignored him. No one on the little island locked the doors to their houses. At least, not until now.

"You don't, do you? Well, let me tell you that Evan's dying left more than one person alone. My father had no job, no boat or anything else after Evan died. He tried to find work, but was so old no one would hire him. The boat was half his you know, and it wasn't insured, so Dad lost everything that day. He did some odd jobs here and there and finally died a broken man. Mom was already dead so it left me to fend for myself and you're the reason why!"

"Me? I never met you before today. Why would you blame me? I didn't cause the storm and certainly didn't want Evan dead. I loved him. I almost died myself when he didn't come back."

"Don't play games with me! You know damned good and well that your daddy had Evan killed. He was dead long before the storm hit that day! Everyone in town knows that."

"Had him killed? What are you talking about? Evan drowned!"

"Graham Stanford paid Robert Chung to kill Evan and burn his boat. You act like you have never heard that before."

Meg stood looking at the stranger in her home with her mouth open. "That's not true and you know it." The words came out of her mouth more loudly than she thought she was capable of.

"It is true. Half the island knew it. Why do you think your dad retired to Corpus Christi right after?"

"To take care of me and Jon."

"Or to hide from the people who knew about Evan?"

Meg was shaking worse than before. Could this man be telling the truth, and what did he want with her after all these years?

"I don't believe you. Get out of my house!"

"This should be my house by all rights. You should be paying me to keep my mouth shut. Your precious family doesn't need this kind of trouble. So, here is what we're gonna' do. I will contact you soon with a bank account number and the expected deposits to be made. We'll talk then about just how much they will be. I know you have the money, so don't call the police or I'll smear your family's name all over south Texas and don't think I won't!"

By the time he had finished speaking his face was close enough to hers that the brim of his hat touched her forehead, she could see his day-old beard, and smell his putrid breath tinged with rum. His eyes bored into her even though she could not see their color in the dark. She shook with fear—not because she was afraid he would smear her family name, but because she was afraid he might smear her, all over the walls. He looked as crazy as his story, and maybe he was. Then he turned on his heel and quickly walked out the unlocked back door, leaving her shaking.

Meg ran to the door to lock the broken latch even though she knew it didn't work. Then she ran to the front door to do the same. She had no idea where the key was that opened those doors, but didn't care. She wasn't going outside anyway.

Immediately she thought of Alex. She had his cell phone number and would call him. Surely, he wasn't still mad at her and would understand how scared she was of the intruder. She dialed his number, but after it rang a dozen times, she got the message. He wasn't going to talk to her anymore.

With no police on the island, her next thought was Jon. No, she couldn't call him with the name Chung hanging over their heads. Besides, she took the last ferry for the day and there wouldn't be another until morning.

"Le Chez," she said as she flipped through the directory for the mainland. She dialed the number and it rang at least six times before someone answered. The background noise made it difficult to hear.

"Hello, is Sam there?"

"Sam is busy, how can I help you?" said the voice on the other end.

"This is, um Meg—he buys my produce in town?" She was unsure how to introduce herself. After all she wasn't a friend or even a patron.

"Sam is busy and we don't need no vegetables tonight." The voice sounded impatient.

"I know Sam is busy, and you don't need vegetables, but I NEED to talk to him. It's an emergency!"

A long, obviously irritated breath came through the phone. "Like I said, Sam is busy."

"Put him on the phone!" Meg yelled into the receiver. She would not be put off again by someone who thought she was unimportant. Her father had treated her like a child until the day he died, but now he was gone.

"Hold a minute." The irritated speaker placed the phone down with a clunk.

Long minutes later a voice came on the other end, "This is Sam, and this had better be good."

"Sam, this is Meg and it's not good. I've been broken into and threatened. I didn't know who else to call. I need help!"

"This is who?"

"Meg! With the vegetables!"

"Sorry Meg, I don't need any vegetables tonight but thanks." The noise in the restaurant increased as someone laughed.

"No wait, don't hang up! I need your help. I'm not selling anything. I've had an intruder at my house and I'm afraid to leave. Please help me!"

"Meg? Are you all right?" He finally understood. "Hold a minute." He walked away from the hustle and bustle of the restaurant. "Okay, I can hear now. Is something wrong? Did you say you had an intruder? Where? At your house?"

Finally, someone understood her. "Yes, he broke into my house and threatened me. I'm sorry to call you but, you were the only person I could think of. Alex didn't answer his phone, and Jon is on the mainland."

"Well, Alex is here having dinner. You hang on, I'll be right there." The phone went dead in her ear.

Chapter 17

Alex was scooping the last of Sam's Louisiana Shrimp Bake into his open mouth when the man behind him leaned his chair back.

"Good stuff, huh?"

Alex wiped his mouth with the napkin. "Oh my God, Sam really outdid himself tonight." Alex smiled with satisfaction.

"It's not Sam—it's his shrimper that's good. Nothin' but the best."

"Who's his shrimper?"

"Well, me of course." Paul smiled.

"Oh Paul, I can't take you anywhere. Leave the poor man alone and let him eat his dinner in peace." The plump woman across the table from Paul smiled as she berated her husband.

Alex turned around to face the man who'd interrupted his dinner. "I'm Alex Wallace." He stuck out his hand.

"Paul Smith. And this here is the little woman, Becky, my wife. You're the artist that just moved to the island." It sounded more like a statement than a question. Small towns.

"That's right, and you own one of those shrimping boats at the dock?"

"I own the only good shrimper around here. I sell to Sam and others who know a good thing when they smell it!"

"How can something that smells so bad, taste so good?" Alex laughed.

"Well, that depends upon what you think smells bad. I happen to think they smell like money!"

"Alex," Sam ran over to his table. "Meg's in trouble."

"What's wrong with Meg?"

"Evening Paul," Sam said quickly, nodding. "Meg just called and said she had an intruder that threatened her. She tried to call you but you didn't answer."

"I left my phone at home accidentally and didn't think anything about it." He stood up from the table.

"Come on, let's go. I told her I'd be right there." Sam jerked his head toward the door.

"Something's wrong with Meg? Then I'm coming too. Honey, I'll see you at home." Paul pecked his wife on the cheek and ran for the door with the others.

****

Meg sat on the couch in the dark, afraid to even turn on a light. The light coming from under the door to the bathroom she was about to use when interrupted, was the only one on in her tiny house.

Hearing voices coming from the sand dunes, she looked up and tightened her grip on the unlit flashlight in her hand. Was the intruder back?

"This way," a familiar voice said, leading the others to the back of the house.

"This garden just keeps getting bigger!"

"Meg!" Someone whispered as the group knocked on the back door.

"Alex?" Meg ran for the door and unfastened the broken latch.

Alex stood in the dark with two men behind him. "I tried to call you. I was afraid you weren't speaking to me!" Meg said as she hugged him, pulling him inside. Behind him on the crooked steps stood Sam Taylor from Le Chez and Paul Smith, the shrimper from down on the dock.

"Sam!" Thank you for coming so quickly." She hugged the chef as he entered.

"What are friends for?" Paul said as the tall man ducked his head coming in the door.

"And Paul! Good grief, Sam you brought reinforcements."

"Well, you have a lot of friends in this town." Sam looked around at the tiny house. "That garden keeps getting bigger! Alex led us around it or I'd still be looking for the house. Do you ever rest, woman? Now tell us what happened. Who was it, and what did he do? Are you sure you're all right?"

"He hangs out at the dock sometimes and has a tugboat. He said his name was Mike, but I don't know for sure. He is often leaning against the shed on the dock with his hat down over his eyes when I'm there,"

"I know who you are talking about," said Paul, "I think his name is Mike Fitzgerald. Nobody likes him. I tried to talk to him once and about all I got was a name. I heard people say he's price gouging customers with the problems in the bay and all the sand this year. He's rakin' in the cash because of other peoples misfortunes."

Alex stood close to Meg like he was afraid she would get away. "What did he say, Meg?" he asked.

What was she going to say? Now that she called Sam to help her, she couldn't lie to him. "Well, he said he knew who I was and he wanted me to pay him. I don't know, I think he mistook me for someone else, but I was still scared. He threatened me and said he would be back later. He thinks he can blackmail me and plans on bringing me an account number to send the money to."

"What do you mean he thought he knew who you were?" Alex asked.

The old house creaked in the wind as the silence hung heavily in the room. Paul cleared his throat and shifted on his feet. "It's all right, Meg, we all know you're a Stanford. We always have. We don't know why you want to hide it, but I'm sure you have your reasons. We don't care what your name is. We just want to be good neighbors."

Meg's heart caught in her throat and she coughed to prevent the flood of tears, but they still welled up in her eyes. These people were her friends. They didn't judge her. They never even asked what her last name was and she never wondered why.

"Stanford. Nice name. I guess I never even asked before. Is that a bad name around here or something?" Alex asked.

Sam and Paul both tried to stifle a laugh and then Sam said, "Not bad, they just own the whole damned place. I mean the whole island and everything in it. I write a check every month to the landlord for rent to the Stanford Corporation," Sam said.

"Stanford Corporation? Like the philanthropy bunch?" Alex looked quizzically at Meg.

"We do fund philanthropy projects," Meg said shyly, "but I haven't been involved in that for years. I gave it over to Jon to handle."

Alex opened his mouth to speak and then thought better of it. "We really need to talk," he said.

"What can we do, Meg?" Sam asked as he looked around. "I have to get back to the restaurant, but I could come back later. Do you think everything is okay?"

"Probably, Sam." Meg looked around. "There's not much to do tonight, but I want to get a lock on the door tomorrow."

"I'll stay with her tonight." Alex put his arm around her and nodded to the other men. "She'll be okay."

Sam hesitated a moment. "All right, but if you need anything, call again," Sam went out the door with Paul in tow and they walked back through the garden and up the hill to the road. Even though Alex was new to the island, he was sure Meg was in good hands.

Chapter 18

After Sam and Paul left, Meg poured two glasses of iced tea and sat them on the table, then looked at Alex.

"How about something a little stronger?" She pulled the Johnnie Walker from the cabinet and poured two more glasses.

"I think the time might be right." Alex grinned.

He clinked his glass against hers. As she sipped, he downed the golden liquid without a word. Then, poured another.

"Do you mind?" He poured without waiting for an answer. "A little liquid courage. I think I owe you an explanation about what I call the Chauncey Factor."

"You don't owe me anything, Alex," Meg began. "I called you tonight."

"Yes, I think I do. I was mad about Jon checking up on me. I guess if I was a son of a single mother who lived alone on an island, I'd be careful too. And he is in a position to find out more than most." He breathed deeply and then continued. "Let me just start by saying, I didn't do it. She was a spoiled little rich girl." He stopped, realizing what he just said, and looked at Meg. She was staring at him over her glass of scotch.

He cleared his throat. "Can we sit down?"

"Of course." She led him to the worn couch in the tiny living room. They sat side-by-side on the small sofa with its back to the window of the porch.

"One more time. I'm not trying to be rude. There's rich and then there's rich. I know now that you and your family have lots of money. I come from a different background. I worked my way through college and had student loans when I came out the other end. But, even though you went to school differently, you and Chauncey are nothing alike. She thought the world should bow down to her whims and I was one of those whims. She tried on more than one occasion to seduce me and when I refused, she retaliated with a sexual assault charge. Of course it went to trial and after she lost, her father had the records sealed. She was of age, so it wasn't a juvenile record, but he had friends that could still get it sealed. Anyway, I was acquitted, but afterward the school decided I was a liability and let me go. That's when I decided to paint for a while and see where it led me. It led me here. I knew about the available grant money, because I helped students get grants. I didn't know until today that the grant had anything to do with you or your family."

Meg stared at the man in front of her a long time. He was the first friend she had made on the island—well, maybe that wasn't true. She found out tonight she had more friends than she realized—but she felt he was a good friend, and was unwilling to let him go. She wanted to believe him.

"I'm surprised that Jon didn't do a background check before he gave out the grant."

"He probably did. I used my mother's maiden name—Simmons—for the grant. I was afraid all the publicity about the trial might keep me from getting it. I was born to a single mother and my name was legally

Simmons. I was never adopted by her husband—my stepfather—but I took his name. I've used the name Wallace all these years. I know it wasn't actually the truth, but I am not sure I was thinking straight when I applied for the grant. I was still running scared. That grant has given me a second chance." He paused and breathed deeply. "I'll pay the money back if you want me to."

"No, of course not," she replied.

"Well, something wonderful happened the other day. I was going to tell you about it, but then I acted like a child and stormed out. I have a buyer for my painting of the ocean I showed you. The one painted in your vegetable juice. This purchaser has a gallery on the mainland and wants me to paint more for a show. It might end up getting my name out and my work seen by a lot of people. Anyway, I could stand to make some money and then I could pay the grant back if you want."

"Like I said, I don't want the money back, and I'm thrilled to know that your art is going places."

He sighed and seemed to relax. "Me too. It's been a long time coming." He picked up her hand. It felt as natural as if they had been together for years.

"So what did this Mike character think he could blackmail you about? Your name?" Alex asked.

"Well, for one thing, he said..." Meg cleared her throat and tried not to cry. "He said that my father had my fiancé killed. I know that is a lie. Evan died at sea. There was a storm the day he went out and he never came back. It happens to fishermen. I had just told Evan I was pregnant and we were planning a wedding. My father was very upset, so we decided we would elope.

He went out alone that day because he needed the money. His partner was sick, but he thought the fishing would be good just prior to the storm. I asked him not to go, but he insisted. He was alone on the boat. I don't know how anyone could have killed him unless they found him out on the ocean. Anyway, my father was angry, but he wasn't stupid. He didn't have Evan killed, I'm sure of that."

"So the heiress was going to run off with the fisherman, huh?"

"Well, when you put it that way! I was planning on marrying the love of my life. We would have made a good life together and raised Jon. But, things got in the way. My father was a hard man. He wanted everything his way, including me and my mother. When I rebelled, he wasn't happy. I was his princess, but I think getting away from here and going to college changed me. He wanted me to be a shipper like him. I wanted other things in life and he disagreed. I know now what it is like to be a parent. Kids don't always turn out like you planned, but they're yours anyway."

"Did Jon turn out like you planned?"

"Well, sometimes I think he did. I also think he has a lot of my father in him. After Evan died and it became obvious that I was pregnant, my family moved back to Corpus Christi and away from the tiny island where everyone thought they knew our business. Mom didn't live long enough to see the grandson that I hoped she would learn to love. All she could see was the shame. Times were different then, and my family ran in Corpus Christi's society circles where daughters didn't have children outside of marriage. Dad closed his little office in the harbor and opened a much larger one on the mainland. It soon became apparent that he owned much more than he let anyone know about, even Mom. He died when Jon was ten and then we inherited it all. I made sure that Jon had everything he needed and the best education money could buy. I always planned to come back to the island once Jon was raised, and I ended up staying on the mainland longer than I should have. The friends I thought I had all along, I found were not really my friends at all. So, when I did move here, I sort of became a hermit. I really didn't plan it that way, I was just running from my past to a place that I loved. You don't know how surprised I was this evening to find out that I had friends on this island. That's the good thing about a small community, people look after each other, even when they know your dubious past."

"Meg, you don't have a dubious past. You just hide out because you think you don't belong. You do." Alex pulled her hand to his lips and kissed it lightly. "No one these days thinks twice about single mothers. I know things have changed in the last thirty years, but the people of Corpus Christi society are still just people. There are good and bad like everywhere else."

He was holding her fingers near his lips and caressing them. She found she didn't mind. The old feelings of running away when someone got too close were somewhere packed away in the back of her brain. She reached up and touched his hand and he looked at her face and smiled. Something inside her opened up and accepted his smile. Something she had not felt for a long time. Maybe it was passion, maybe it was friendship, or maybe it was just a connection with another human being. She had a feeling of letting go of the worries of everyday life when he kissed her gently on the mouth the first time. He sat back looking at her and smiled, pushing the hair from around her face. The second kiss was more urgent, but she didn't pull away, she allowed it to engulf her as she sighed and relaxed, exhaling. Could she have actually found a soul mate again? Twice in one lifetime? Or was she just starved for affection and would take anything that was offered after all these years? She found she didn't care as he unbuttoned her blouse and kissed her neck.

Chapter 19

Mike Fitzgerald sat at his desk in the efficiency apartment he had finally rented in Corpus Christi. Some nights he stayed on the tug, but tonight he felt like going home. So, he paid a local guy with a boat to take him to the mainland after the ferry had quit running for the night. He felt like a weight had been lifted and good days were right around the corner. He would get Meg to pay for his silence and then when he had enough money, he would leave the island without a word to anyone. An offshore account could be set up and payments could be made forever to a fake name and address. No one cared in the Bahamas. Offshore accounts had become common business practice these days.

On the old computer he bought used, he printed out the paperwork from the account online and placed it in the folder. Then he wrote the account and bank number on a slip of paper he would put in the envelope for Meg. She didn't need all the particulars—she could just have the deposit set up for him. No need to get greedy, she might involve the authorities. Five thousand a month should do it. Sixty thousand a year tax free could be a comfortable living, especially in the Caribbean. Maybe he would find some little fishing village where he was king. He could put the boat to work for him too. Tugs were needed everywhere.

He scrawled her name across the envelope as he took another swig from the cheap rum bottle and then lay down on the filthy sheets of the single bed and drifted off. But, not before setting an alarm so he could meet the guy with the boat to take him back to the island before dawn.

****

When Meg woke, daylight was beginning to break through the clouds and a light breeze blew salty ocean smells through her bedroom window. The unfamiliar snoring startled her at first and then she remembered. She turned to see the brownish-gray hair poking out from under her antique quilt and lightly touched Alex's freckled shoulder. His scent engulfed her as he slept soundly without stirring. Something about last night seemed so natural and normal it surprised her. She expected to feel fear or at least embarrassment. After all, it had been years since she had slept with a man, but all she felt was comfortable. Comfort with a man she barely knew seemed out of place, but she smiled. Maybe it was the fact that they shared their lives last night—or maybe it was because he made her feel safe with all the problems that had recently cropped up in her life, but he felt as comfortable as warm sweats on a cold day.

Carefully, she slid out of bed, reaching for the robe that lay across the foot, and wrapped it around her. Closing the bedroom door, she padded softly into the kitchen. She poured water into the coffee pot, measured the grounds into the basket and turned it on. There on the floor in front of the kitchen door was an envelope with her name on it. She reached for the envelope, wondering if someone had dropped it the night before.

It was seldom that she had company in her kitchen, but last night there were three. Three new friends, she thought with a smile as she opened the envelope. Inside was a single piece of paper with hand-written numbers on it. Confused at first, the fog of sleep began to lift and she realized it was the blackmail note—as promised. Mike Fitzgerald had been at her door again as she slept. The door that didn't lock. A shudder ran through her at first, and then anger. She stood up straight. This man was trying to take advantage of her. Who did he think he was? One thing was for certain, before she slept again, all the doors and windows in her beach house would lock.

"What's for breakfast?" asked the sleepy voice behind her. Alex stood barefoot wearing only his jeans and a smile as he ran a hand through his hair. Then he looked at her quizzically. "Is everything okay?"

The smell of coffee filled the room and the sound of waves rolling relentlessly on the shore floated through the open windows. "There was an envelope under the door this morning." She handed him the paper.

"What is it?"

"It looks like routing and account numbers and that is an amount." She pointed to the dollar sign on the paper. "Mike Fitzgerald was at my door again last night. Can you install a lock? I mean if you can't I am sure Mr. Sanders from the hardware store can. Maybe I should pay him to check all the locks."

"I'll get with him and we'll get it done. Are you okay? You look a little rattled. I think we need to involve the police. This is getting serious. The guy was at your house twice in one night!"

"Or early this morning. Either way, you may be right. Maybe it is time to call the police."

Alex pulled the cell phone from his pocket and dialed 911, then walked into the living room as she poured two cups of coffee. She sat his on the coffee table and said quietly. "I'm taking a shower." She walked toward the bathroom with her coffee. It was so unlike her to let someone else handle her problems. But, somehow, it just seemed right.

"The police are on their way." Alex was in the bedroom when she walked in to get dressed. "They're sending a detective out, but it will take a while to get here on the ferry. They aren't running with lights and sirens."

"They don't need to. But, thanks for helping me get this started. I might have not done anything if I hadn't had some help." And she pulled the sundress over her head as he watched.

Alex smiled and stepped toward her, lightly kissing her on the lips. "Thank you for last night. It has been a long time, and I don't know about you, but it just felt right."

Meg smiled. "I should be thanking you. It did feel right. It has been a long time since I let anyone into my life. It probably was a mistake for me to wait so long, but I just closed up after Evan died, and concentrated on Jon. It's nice to have someone around if just to make a phone call for me." She smiled and kissed him back. Over his shoulder she saw a shadow through the window and jumped.

"Jon," she said and hurried to the door. This was going to be awkward, but maybe it was time to put all the cards on the table about Alex—and the blackmailing. It was time he knew what had been going on in her life.

"Hi sweetie, come in." She opened the door to her only son.

"Hi, Mom. Coffee smells good." He handed her a box of cinnamon rolls.

"Let me get you some." She poured him a cup of coffee as Alex walked out of the bedroom with his shirt on this time.

Jon stopped with the cup halfway to his lips.

"Good morning, Jon." Alex walked into the kitchen. He did his best to act natural about the strained situation.

"Alex." Jon set down the coffee and eyed first his mother then Alex again. "You're here early."

"I was here all night. Your mother has had a problem."

"Mom? Is everything okay?"

"Let's sit." She pulled out the chair at the kitchen table.

Jon turned the chair around and straddled it, eyeing them both. "What's wrong?"

Meg looked at Alex, who nodded at her to tell her story. "I've been having some trouble with a man on the dock." She handed him the envelope. Jon opened it and took out the piece of paper.

"Account numbers?"

"Yes, he is trying to blackmail me. We've called the police."

"I assume we've all handled this paper?" Jon said, putting it back in its envelope.

"Yes."

"Well, we've probably ruined any evidence that

was on it. Now tell me what this is about. What man at the dock?"

"There has been a man at the dock lately that I've seen many times, but never spoken to until recently. I talked to Paul Smith, the shrimper, and he told me his name was Mike Fitzgerald. He said he was Rowdy Fitzgerald's son."

"Who is Rowdy Fitzgerald?"

"He was your father's fishing partner. They owned a boat and fishing business together. I remember meeting Rowdy once, but didn't know if he had any children. However, Fitzgerald has been bothering me when I go to the dock to trade for shrimp—just talking to me as I go past and making me nervous. He acted in a threatening manner even though he didn't say much. Then he said he knew who I was and knew who killed Evan."

"I thought Dad died in a storm."

"Well, me too, but he says that Evan was murdered." She couldn't finish the sentence with 'your grandfather had him murdered.'

"Okay. I don't understand why anyone would think that my dad was murdered, and why after thirty years would they bring it up now?"

"That's what I wondered, but he has decided to blackmail me. Jon, he says that your grandfather had Evan killed."

"What! That's ridiculous."

"He said that he knows who did it and he wanted money to keep quiet or he would smear the family name."

Jon stood and began to pace the tiny kitchen. "Well, let him smear! I wonder if he has ever heard of a defamation of character lawsuit? This is not happening. We're going to find this Mike guy and shut his mouth once and for all. He is not going to threaten you with poison pen notes. How did he get this to you, anyway?"

"It was slid under the door this morning."

"He was in her house," Alex began, "after dark last night. He broke in and threatened her face to face."

Jon paused, then looked at his mother and then Alex and glared. "So you decided to be the knight in shining armor and spend the night with my mother to keep her safe?"

"Jon!"

"Mom, have you thought about the fact that all this trouble started just as Alex showed up? Maybe he has something to do with it."

"I can't believe you said that!"

"Well, the timing is right. I mean about the time that Alex shows up, so does Fitzgerald."

"You're wrong. Alex has been trying to help. He called the police for me. The detectives are coming out. But, you know it takes a while with the ferry and such."

"Okay, pack a bag. As soon as the police leave, you're coming home with me. This is just one more reason why you can't live here alone. It takes the damned police an hour to get here! At least in Corpus Christi I'll know you're okay. And then the police can find Mike Fitzgerald and put him where he belongs."

"I'm not living in a high-rise apartment in Corpus Christi. I know you're trying to help, but I'm an adult and can take care of myself."

"No, you can't. Just look at how you have made a mess of your life! Living off a vegetable patch, trying to be a recluse because some old boyfriend died thirty years ago? Those days are over. Evan isn't coming back. You can quit sitting on the seashore waiting. He's dead!"

Meg looked at the man in front of her. Her son that she had raised lovingly had the same look on his face as her father used to when he told her how she should live her life. She wanted to lash out. She wanted to hurt him like he hurt her.

"Fitzgerald said the man that killed Evan was Robert Chung, Victoria's uncle." The words hung in the air like a shroud, covering everything it touched.

"Okay, that's the last straw," Jon said quietly as someone rapped on the door.

Meg looked up and saw two men in suits at her front door. She walked to the door and opened it.

"Meg Stanford?" the first one said.

"Yes," Meg said quietly.

"I'm Detective Arnold and this is Detective Samuels of the Corpus Christi police." They both showed her their badges. "May we come in?"

"Of course." Meg ushered the men into her already crowded kitchen. "This is my son, Jon Stanford, and my friend Alex Wallace. He is the one that called you. Would you like a cup of coffee?"

"No thank you ma'am, we're fine. Just tell us what has occurred so far." Detective Arnold was a young man about Jon's age. Everyone seemed young to Meg these days. The other detective looked around her house as she and Arnold talked. She wondered if he was listening at all. However, when she spoke about Mike breaking into her house his ears perked up like he was actually listening for the first time. Then he took the envelope with the scrap of paper and put them into a plastic bag. After taking everyone's name and phone number, they excused themselves and promised to be in touch.

"I don't know how much good that did," Jon said. "I hope they follow through. Are you going to pack that bag and go home with me?"

"No. I'm staying here. Alex and Mr. Sanders at the hardware store are going to install a lock on the back door and check the rest of them in the house."

"Mom, a lock isn't going to do you much good if someone really wants in. This place is falling apart. A gust of wind could knock it over."

Meg stood her ground, "No, I'm staying."

Jon shook his head slowly. "You know where I am if you need me, not that I could get here very fast." He turned on his heel to leave then turned back around. "I'd better not find out you're involved in this," he said, pointing to Alex, and stomped out the door.

"I'm sorry," Meg said to Alex after Jon left. She couldn't believe her son could act the way he did. It was like he was three years old and jealous of his mother's boyfriend. Did she just think boyfriend? Was that what Alex was becoming? After all, they did sleep together last night. But, whatever the relationship with Alex was, she had never been so angry at Jon. She wasn't an invalid that needed a nursing home. She had taken care of herself and him all their lives and now this was how he treated her.

"No. No need to apologize. If I were in his shoes, I might feel the same. Let's go get that lock and see what we can do about this door."

"No, I'll stay here and finish up some things. If you wouldn't mind taking care of that for me, I would appreciate it. After all the activity around here recently, I'm sure that Fitzgerald will stay away for a while."

Alex paused and looked at Meg quizzically. "If you're sure. I'll be back as soon as possible."

After Alex and Jon left, Meg looked around her cottage. Her home suddenly felt like a prison with the impending locks on the door and a son who tried to look after her only to make her feel like a child. Stepping into the bedroom, she opened the door to the closet. The new outfits were still in the bag from her trip to Corpus Christi. She had not hung them up. With the humidity, she planned to take them to the cleaners before wearing them again.

She walked to the front of the house and looked out into the ocean. Kicking off her shoes on the front porch, she padded barefoot to the shore. The breeze blew through her hair as she watched the shorebirds in their endless race with the waves—back and forth they ran. She felt like those birds, always running this way and that to avoid getting her feet wet in the ocean of life.

She might never go to the mainland again, she thought as she remembered the looks at the salon and now her son's attitude. This was why she left. Taking the beautiful new outfits from her bag, she flung them into the tide as it rushed out. The pink, green and coral colors muted as they mixed with the sea-green water. Never again. She watched as they washed out to sea. They could have a wedding without her.

Chapter 20

Still standing ankle deep in water and looking out at the sea, Meg thought back to the time she was a young woman ruled over by her arrogant father, and to the reasons she never wanted to go back to her old life. She was wearing the silk peach dress with dyed-to-match satin pumps and was sure her mother would have loved it. It would not have been her choice. The house she and her parents had moved to in Corpus Christi was a large two-story overlooking the harbor. It had been built when air conditioning was not even a thought in the builder's mind. The overly large windows faced the water and caught the breeze as it blew in off the ocean.

Jon was downstairs watching a movie and playing with toy cars. The nanny was in for the evening. Meg was attending another boring dinner with her overbearing father again. He wanted to show her off to his customers and he had insisted she wear the dress he picked out for her. He still thought she might take over for him someday. She hated these dinners, but Graham Stanford didn't take no for an answer—even from his daughter.

Since her mother's death, Meg felt she replaced her in some ways. Graham insisted she accompany him and she always did as she was told, even though secretly she hated the dinners and possibly her father.

"Meg, you ready?" Graham called from the

hallway.

"Coming." She picked up the evening bag that lay on the bed and walked from the room.

Her father stood in the hallway in a tailor-made tuxedo that fit his apple shape. She told him it made him look slimmer because that is what he wanted to hear. In reality that was an impossible task for any tailor. His shape, age, diet, and alcohol consumption made him ripe for a heart attack. She smelled him as she walked past and knew he had already been into the scotch.

"Mitch and the car are already out front." She walked into the living room to kiss her son goodbye. He was on the rug with a fire truck and a cartoon movie on the TV.

"Not too many snacks," Meg said to the nanny, leaning over to kiss Jon. "Love you, kiddo."

"Love you too," he said automatically, never looking up.

The car was at the front door and the driver stood with the door open for Meg and her father's entrance. He leered at Meg as she went past. She hated the way he looked at her and wondered why her father hired him in the first place. She guessed he was someone who owed her father money and that was his way of keeping an eye on him. His employees were often people he had beat in the business world and were forever dependent upon Graham for a living now.

The country club had a large valet entrance with columns on either side of massive carved doors that must have weighed a ton each. She hated the country club and all it stood for, but loved the look of an Italian villa the building had copied. Maybe she would travel to Tuscany someday to see a real one. Once inside, the music and wine were flowing as people chattered about their latest trip to Paris or business deal.

As soon as Meg and Graham arrived, she was left alone to mingle until dinner as her father went off to talk business with someone else. Miranda, her only friend at these gala events, was nowhere in sight. Usually, they sat in a corner and talked until dinner when they reunited with their families. Miranda was a little younger than Meg, but disliked the country club dinners as much as she did. Her husband insisted she attend and then left her to fend for herself. That was how she and Meg first met, at the bar sitting alone.

Meg walked to the bar and ordered a glass of wine, looking for her friend and when she didn't find her, she stood with her back to the bar, surveying the crowd. Amy, in a jade green dress that looked two sizes too small, and her entourage were zeroing in on her as they walked her way.

Amy was the wife of one of her father's competitors and felt it was her duty to make sure everyone followed the rules. Her rules. She was like the kid on the playground that managed to draw up sides and pick the players in the game. A game that she invented and only she knew the rules. She always made a point of making sure Meg knew she was the odd man out. She didn't have a husband or even a mother. She was adrift in the society that had taken over the shipping business. Meg was the little kid that was never chosen for the ballgame and Amy was the bully that called the shots. And so it was this night as many others.

"Meg!" Amy glided up and made fake kissing

noises on either side of Meg's face. "So good to see you. Are you alone? Where's Graham?"

"He's here somewhere." Meg took a sip of her wine. She would not let this woman make a mockery of her again.

"How is that little boy of yours?" Amy asked with a wicked smile. "What is his name again?"

"Jon." Meg's face began to burn more from anger than embarrassment. Amy knew Jon's name as well as she knew his mother's. And experience told Meg where this conversation was going.

"Of course. He's about the same age as my Jeremy. They go to school together, don't they?"

"You know they do." Meg readied herself for the worst.

"Well, you don't have to get huffy. I've always been surprised that they let him in the school with a single mother. But, money can get you anything."

Meg stared at the woman in the green dress. Her first thought was to walk away, but she was talking about Jon, and Meg's maternal instincts kicked in.

"I don't know what his mother's marital status has to do with his education. Jon is an excellent student— the head of his class—and not a bully like your Jeremy."

"Bully!" Amy said, trying to hide a smile. She was probably proud of the fact that he followed in his mother's shoes. It was obvious that Amy was in charge in her family. Her husband was a mere figure-head. But, Meg was sure little Jeremy was planning a coup in the near future. Even his mother was not going to stop him from taking over. "My son is not a bully. If you are talking about the incident with the history book, Jeremy wasn't involved in that."

****

Jon came home one day without his history book and said it was lost when she questioned him about his homework. He told her he needed a new one. Meg knew something was wrong with the boy as soon as he came in the door. He was too quiet. She gave him a snack and sat at the bar with him, waiting for the story to come out. Eventually, it did. Jeremy and some boys from school had taken the history book and torn it up after Jon had aced the test. They didn't like someone else being the head of the class, and it was a warning for him to stay in his place.

Meg called the school and went to bat for her son. She knew which kids were responsible for the theft of the book and she planned to make her mark. After all, if she didn't stand up for Jon, who would? Her complaints mostly fell on deaf ears until Graham got involved. He threatened the school board and had Jeremy moved to another class and away from Jon. Then he came home and threatened his grandson, telling him it was time to toughen up and he would not continue to fight the child's battles. After that, Jon did not tell Meg much that went on at school and Graham's lesson hit home. Jon did toughen up. He became more introverted and pulled away from the grandfather he had previously adored.

****

"I'm not arguing with you about an incident that is over and done with." Meg drained her glass and ordered another.

"Taking after your father, I see," Amy said, gesturing to the bar as Meg took the glass from the bartender.

"Well, better than taking after your father," Meg shot back. Amy's father was in a federal prison on tax evasion and was never spoken of in polite circles. Amy quickly married after her father was arrested and seldom let anyone know her maiden name. She cut all ties with her family and hadn't seen her father since he embarrassed the family by getting caught.

The splash came as a surprise and it was several seconds before Meg realized Amy had thrown her drink in her face. She stood with her back to the bar, dripping chardonnay off her chin and onto her dress, not sure how to react, when the noise in the other room became louder.

"Call an ambulance!" someone shouted and all eyes were drawn to the other side of the room.

"Graham Stanford's having a heart attack!" another guest yelled, running up to the bar. "Quick, call 911!"

Meg turned and rushed toward the father that she hated just as Amy lunged at her. Graham lay on the floor on the other side of the huge room. She heard shouts behind her and the barstools fell over as Amy tumbled to the ground, but she could not have cared less. She had to get to Graham. Was he having a heart attack like the man said as she raced to his side?

The rest of the evening was a blur of paramedics, ambulances, IV's, and heart monitors. Meg rode to the hospital in the ambulance with Graham, and he was taken to the cardiac unit of the ICU.

Meg called the nanny and told her to stay with Jon and she would come home soon. She stayed all night beside Graham's bed and held his swollen hand with the needle sticking out of it. Graham lived in the hospital almost a week before he expired. He was alone and Meg at home with Jon when it happened. The doctor called to tell her he had done all he could for Graham, and Meg found she had no tears left for the man who ruled over her and Jon for so many years.

After the funeral, Mitch drove Meg and Jon back to the house. She fired the chauffeur as soon as he dropped them off. She would no longer tolerate his attitude. The next day, she called the lawyers and began the process of taking over Graham's business. She was sure there would be more firings in the days ahead when she found out how the business was run. That was when the idea of philanthropy started to germinate in her mind. Maybe she could do some good with the money her father left to her and Jon.

"Allen Simpson," Meg said to the receptionist that answered the phone. "Yes, this is Meg Stanford." Allan was a friend from school who had gone on to work for one of the most prestigious law firms in Corpus. She hoped to retain him to help her reorganize the family fortune into a philanthropy project.

"Meg! How great to hear from you. And I'm so sorry to hear about Graham. Is there anything I can do for you and Jon?" Allen spoke with sincere empathy as he queried his old friend.

"Good to talk to you too, Allen, and as a matter of fact there may be something you can do for us. I was wondering if I could get an appointment to discuss the corporation with you. As the Chairman now that Graham is gone, I want to make some changes and you are just the person I need to see to those changes." She spoke the rehearsed speech in one breath.

"Well, that is a mouthful. You want to make

changes to the corporation. Don't you have in-house counsel?"

"I did. I fired him, and I need someone new to help me lead this corporation in a new direction."

In the months to come, Meg and Allen had a forensic accountant go over the books with a fine-tooth comb. A complete turn-over of many of the long-time employees took place, and a new corporation was set up to fund philanthropy projects around the world. A portion was set in trust for her and Jon, and Allen made partner when he brought in his latest, and very rich, client. He became a fixture at the offices of the Stanford Corporation and became a great influence on Jon becoming an attorney as he grew into a man.

Allen and his wife Sammy were good friends over the years who could always be counted on in an emergency, until the day that Allen slumped over after a massive stroke not long after Jon became an associate at the same firm. He was her friend and a mentor to her son—and then he was gone.

Chapter 21

The lock on the door replaced, Alex and Mr. Sanders—whose first name, she'd learned, was Bill—checked the rest of the house. Meg thought how foolish she was all these years never getting to know her neighbors. Maybe soon she should ask them over for her famous gumbo and cornbread. At least, Jon thought it could be famous. One way or another, she had friends and she needed to show her appreciation. She had been alone long enough. Time to try her wings again, maybe. As a young woman she never met a stranger. That was probably how she was so open to Evan. Her mother always tried to teach Meg to be more reserved until she really got to know people. Her outgoing personality was just one more thing that her mother disliked about her daughter. But, she had closed the door to friends over the years.

"I think you're good to go, Meg," Bill said, picking up his toolbox. "Now if you open the windows, and I know you always do, it's still easy enough to get in. The little hook on the screens won't keep anyone out. A pocket knife will make short work of them."

With no air conditioning, Meg always counted on cross-ventilation to cool the little house.

"Well, at least it won't be as easy to get in as it was when there was no working lock on the back door. I can't believe it has come to this. I've never locked my doors on this island."

"Most people lock their doors, Meg," Alex said. "It is just standard practice. I'm sure you locked yours when you lived in Corpus Christi."

"Well, in Corpus Christi yes, but not here."

"I lock my doors," Bill said. "The wife insists. She's not from here and she sleeps better when things are locked up."

"I lock mine too," Alex replied. "The store gets locked anytime I'm not there."

"Well, I guess I will too now." Meg thought it was interesting how she had gone from an open heart to a locked door. When she was young and carefree she locked her doors—everyone did. Now that she was older it was her heart that was locked instead of her doors. Maybe she needed to rethink her priorities. Last night Alex helped to unlock her heart and now for safety's sake she would begin to lock her doors once more. It seemed like a small tradeoff.

"Weather service says a tropical storm is forming out in the Gulf that looks like it might turn into a major hurricane. Are you ready, Meg? Got boards for your windows and an emergency bag packed? I guess you go into Corpus Christi to be with your son. The wife has already gassed up the car and has our bags packed. She doesn't like hurricanes and we'll be leaving town at the first wind gust."

"I guess I hadn't heard. I don't watch much TV or listen to the radio very often."

"We'll get ready," Alex said.

"I've still got some plywood at the store if you need any, Meg."

"I'll look, Bill, but there was some in the storage

shed on the side of the house. Now, what do I owe you?"

"You don't owe me anything. Alex here bought the lock and so you can settle up with him."

"No really, you came all the way out here and I owe you for your time and trouble."

"Just being neighborly, and it's not that far out here."

"Well, I feel I owe you something."

Bill looked out into the lush garden, "Well, if you really want to do something, the wife and I would love one of your homemade blackberry cobblers when you have the time. But, only if you have the time."

"I'll make the time." Meg smiled. Now that Le Chez was buying most of her vegetables, she had more time on her hands than she used to. Sometimes Sam even picked the produce up and she didn't have to pull her wagon into town. Business was good, but more importantly, she had another friend.

Chapter 22

Meg picked up the silver sugar bowl and turned it around in her hands. It had an ornately carved "S" on the side. Her mother always told her it was a wedding gift from a wealthy land owner in Corpus Christi who was invited to their wedding. It was a cherished possession of her mother's and one that Meg had used for years. It didn't look like much, tarnished and used daily, but it was all she had left of her mother. When Alice Stanford had quietly taken the entire bottle of sleeping pills that were prescribed to her for insomnia after they moved to Corpus Christi, Meg's father had cleaned everything out of the house that was hers. It was as if he was glad she was dead and he didn't have to deal with her anymore. When in reality he probably couldn't bring himself to see her things when he woke up each morning. They had lived together a long time.

Meg had quickly picked up the bowl and taken it to her bedroom to use for a jewelry container as her father cleaned out the house and he was never the wiser. It sat on her dresser for years with the silver clip Mariam had given her to hold back her hair. Possessions from the two women in her life that meant the most to her sat together in the same place. She wondered if Victoria would appreciate the sugar bowl for a wedding present. Meg often dreamed of being able to pass it down to a daughter-in-law someday. She would polish it later and see if she could get all the tarnish off from years of use.

Meg was dusting the coffee table when she saw a flash of light from the road. A tall thin woman casually climbed out of her luxury car in alligator pumps and a pale blue dress, towing her matching purse and valise after her. Her clothes and shoes seemed out of place at the beach. But, she walked to the edge of the sand, kicked off her shoes and carried them the rest of the way. She was no newcomer to beach life.

Meg watched as the shadow stepped up to the door of the front porch and the young woman stood taking off her sunglasses and preparing to knock. Victoria was at her door—and she was alone. What was she doing here? Jon wasn't with her. He would have come through the kitchen door without knocking.

Meg sat down her cleaning supplies, smoothed her hair and opened the door, "Victoria! Please come in. I'm so surprised to see you. I didn't know you were coming."

"Hello, Meg." Victoria swooped in the door, kissing Meg lightly on each cheek. "What a lovely home."

"Well, it needs a little work, but I love the location." Meg was suddenly insecure about her surroundings.

"I hope it is okay to drop by, I didn't have your phone number."

"Of course. You're family."

"Well, almost." Victoria smiled.

"Could I get you something to drink? Maybe some iced tea?" Meg ushered the younger woman into the living room. "Please have a seat and I'll be right back." Meg didn't wait for an answer. Her mother taught her you always offered a guest a beverage.

Victoria sat on the worn couch and looked around the tiny house. "Have you lived here long?" Meg poured two glasses of tea and placed them on a tray with the silver sugar bowl and a plate of cookies.

"Only a few years. My family owned the house for a long time and I have wonderful childhood memories of this place. So, I moved out here from Corpus Christi a few years ago. But, I guess Jon has already told you that. Cookie?"

"Oh no, I'm trying to watch what I eat, at least until the wedding. The dress I have is so fitted, I can't afford to gain an ounce. And that's the main reason for my visit. I brought some designs to show you for the wedding party. I am sure Jon has told you we've moved the wedding date up and we only have about a month to be ready."

Meg's mouth dropped open in surprise. A month! When did this happen and why? "No, Jon hadn't mentioned it to me. But, the last time he was here we talked about other things than the wedding."

"Yes, I heard about the potential blackmail—but I'm sure the Corpus Christi police will take good care of the situation." Victoria opened her valise and displayed swatches and drawings of dresses for the upcoming nuptials. On the first page was a floor length silver-white dress with chiffon overlay that hugged every curve. Victoria was right, you couldn't afford to gain an ounce in a dress like that. The almost backless dress had covered buttons down the back of the skirt and a long chiffon train that Meg was sure was detachable so she could move around at the reception welcoming her guests.

"Beautiful." Meg held the book in her hands. "Did you design it yourself?"

"Of course," Victoria said smugly. "And here are the rest of the wedding party designs. There will be eight bridesmaids and groomsmen, and here are the Mother of the Bride and Mother of the Groom dresses. If you'll let me take some measurements, I'll get started on yours."

Meg looked at the lovely designs in iridescent purple chiffon for the eight bridesmaids and all she could see were the clothes floating in the ocean just a few days ago. Evidently, iridescent was all the rage in Corpus Christi this year. The mother's dresses were matronly, however. She had never met Victoria's mother, but something about the purple silk suits—that still had an iridescent sheen—would have looked better on the Queen of England. She wondered if there was a pill-box hat. No, she would not be wearing that anywhere and besides, she might not be going to the wedding.

Meg cleared her throat, "Now when did you say the wedding was and where?"

"In about a month, Hon, so there's no time to waste! Let me just get a few measurements."

"And where is it taking place? Jon hasn't told me anything."

"Men." Victoria pulled her tape measure from her bag. "The wedding itself will be rather intimate at a cathedral which only holds four hundred, but the reception will be at the country club so there will be plenty of room for everyone. Not every guest will receive an invitation to the wedding, some will only be invited to the reception. Now if you wouldn't mind holding your arms up so I can get a waist measurement."

"It must be a huge event," Meg said, not raising her arms.

"It's the biggest!" Victoria reached for Meg's arm. She smiled as Meg pulled away. "Now here is what I want you to do, I will sit you on Jon's side of the table—oh, and I almost forgot, will you be bringing a plus one? I need a head count for the dinner."

"A plus one?" Meg wasn't sure she understood. "You mean do I have a date? Well, today is the first day I've really heard much about the wedding and you still haven't told me what day it is."

"It is July 30th on a Saturday night. We have room reservations for all the guests at a hotel in Corpus Christi so you will have a place to stay for a couple of nights and not have to be back at the ferry at any certain time. Oh, and I've made appointments for the wedding party to have their hair, nails, and makeup done the afternoon before the wedding, so we'll need you to come early that day. Of course, Jon and I will be leaving the next morning after the wedding for Paris."

"Paris! I'm surprised Jon didn't mention that."

"Well, we really haven't discussed it, he is so busy, you know, with trying to make partner."

"He's making partner? And why don't you think you should mention it to him? I mean what if the partners decide he can't be gone?"

"On his honeymoon? I mean really, how could they say no?"

"Well, they expect a lot from a young associate. And I didn't know he was trying to make partner just yet."

"Of course he'll make partner. Why else would he be there? Now if you will please just stand still and raise your arms."

It sounded like more of a demand than a request and Meg found she didn't respond to demands very well these days. This woman was not the demure little thing that Meg first thought she was.

"Victoria, how old do you think I am?"

"I'm sorry, what?"

"I'll tell you. I'm fifty years old—that's not a child but not old enough to be in a nursing home. I don't like being told what to do, where to be, and most of all what to wear. I respect your designing skills. Your dress and the bridesmaid dresses are lovely. But, the mother's dresses look like they should be worn by an eighty year old. I don't see me wearing that suit anywhere. Maybe I should just find something for myself."

"What? Of course you'll wear the suit. My mother is wearing it and so will you!"

"No, I won't wear the suit. Don't bother to make it for me. IF I come to the wedding, and at this point, it is a big if, I'll find something to wear that is more suitable for my tastes."

"Your tastes! Your tastes have no place here. This is MY wedding and you will wear—and do—what I say."

"You obviously don't know me very well. I don't take well to demands."

"Jon told me you might be hard to handle, but I never thought..." she stood with her hands on her hips, her voice trailing off. Her face became darker and she let out a long breath of air. "Well, I'll just talk to Jon about this. Thank you for the tea," she said, scooping up her designs into the valise and stomping to the door.

"Don't forget your shoes." Meg followed her to the door with the pumps in hand. She smiled. That felt good.

Chapter 23

"That woman is impossible!" Victoria paced the tiny room.

"Have a drink, it will all be over with soon enough." Mike Fitzgerald slid the cheap rum across the tiny table in her direction. It sat next to a cloudy glass that could have been considered clean in some circles.

Victoria walked to the sink, washed and dried the glass, held it up to the dim yellow light and then filled it to the top with rum.

"You didn't use to be so picky," Fitzgerald said.

"I didn't use to be an heiress."

"Not yet, you're not. You have to get him to the altar first, and not getting his momma there is hurtin' your chances."

"You don't think he'd back out now do you? Over his mom's pigheadedness?"

"Pigheadedness? I'm not sure that is a word that an heiress would use. In fact, I'm not sure it's even a word."

"Well, it's the right word for her."

"Just remember he's a momma's boy—and don't scare him off! Now get over here cousin. I haven't seen you in ages."

She smiled. "I'm not your cousin."

"As far as we know." He pulled her down onto the dirty single bed.

They had grown up on the island together even though he considered her just the little girl down the street. He lost track of her when she moved away. But, that night after a few drinks they ended up back at his place. She complained that Sandhill Island always dragged her down. She wasn't going to live her life as a nobody on a tiny island where she was just the daughter of a bankrupt shipper. That was the beginning of the idea they concocted to marry Victoria to Jon's fortune. On the surface, Victoria was a successful fashion designer. She was talented as a designer, but not as a business woman. Her shop was in trouble financially due to some poor investment and business choices. She needed the money. And after the wedding, and a respectable amount of time, Jon would be disposable. If there was a child he would have to leave everything to her and the baby.

Fitzgerald, however, had other plans that didn't involve Victoria's marriage. He knew he couldn't trust her to pay him, even though he was helping her get to Jon's fortune.

Victoria's father died a pauper and he always blamed his misfortunes on the shrewd business practices of Graham Stanford. Both of them in the shipping business on the tiny island, Stanford had weaseled his way out of every business deal they ever made and slowly, but surely, scooped up each square inch of real estate on the island, finally running Chung out of business.

The Fitzgeralds and the Chungs were working families on the island like most everyone else. The Stanfords, however, owned everything and rent was due to them each month for homes and businesses.

Mike Fitzgerald remembered Victoria's cousin Robert Chung from his childhood, and he was always trouble. He was the cause of most of the problems on the island and that was why Mike admired him. Being younger than Robert, Mike looked up to him and his "bad boy" image. Robert and his friends made their livelihood stealing anything or swindling anyone. Just a younger and less successful image of Graham Stanford—Robert lived his life on the edge.

Then came the day that Graham Stanford offered money to Robert Chung to kill Evan—quietly, so it looked like an accident. After the accident, Robert was to leave the island and never return. Knowing Graham's propensity for not paying, Robert got his money up front with a bonus due at the end. He never saw his bonus. But, with the deed done he left in case the authorities got wind that the accident wasn't really an accident.

"You know," Victoria said, lying on her stomach in Fitzgerald's bed tracing the hair on his chest with her finger, "he may want a pre-nup. I mean, he is a lawyer after all and knows what divorce could do to him."

"I thought you had that covered." Fitzgerald placed his forearm behind his neck and propped up on the wall behind the bed.

"Well, I convinced him to move the wedding up and we only have a month—but still, at the last minute he could come up with the paperwork. What will I do then?"

"Tell him you're pregnant? I am sure you could manage something, Victoria. You're very convincing. Anyway, I did my part. I got you two together. I forged the invitation to the country club to get you in."

"You did. However, I've done everything else. I seduced him and pursued him until he thought he did it himself. He was easy, actually—and not a bad lay— but, still, it hasn't all been roses. He's moody and like you said, a momma's boy. If I can just get past her, I'm sure things will go well."

"I've been doing some searching around and think I can find someone to get rid of him when the time is right. You just have to make sure that he keeps control of the Philanthropy Corporation and not Meg. You need to get in on that as soon as possible after the marriage."

"His assistant is Joan. I've met her and I think we should go to lunch or something so we can get to know each other better. Then I can get access to his calendar and find out when the meetings are. There's also more to the fortune than just philanthropy—there are real estate holdings and I don't know what all. I'm sure it is all set up in a trust—I just need to make sure that I'm included in that trust. Meg wanted all the money to go to charity. Jon is not so charitable. He's more sensible. I think I can make him see my way of thinking, especially if there's a baby involved."

She sat up on the side of the bed and reached for the panties on the floor. She stood, pulling them on and then fastened her bra. The dress was still hanging on the chair where he tossed it. Fitzgerald, still propped up on one arm, smiled at her as she dressed. Beautiful, intelligent, and as ruthless as he was; they made a good pair. Now if he could just trust her.

Chapter 24

"You're getting married in a month?" Meg asked her son on her cell phone as she pointed out ripe vegetables to the chef. Sometimes Sam came to her garden to pick his own produce and paid her handsomely. He even purchased his own wagon from the hardware store after pulling hers back and forth a few times. His new green metal wagon pulled much easier than her old wooden one, but she still thought hers had more charm.

"You know how women are about changing their minds." Jon loved poking at his mother when he got the chance.

"You know, you really should tell me these things when they happen and not leave me surprised by a visit from my future daughter-in-law."

"I hear you two didn't get along very well."

"She was a little pushy and you know I don't respond well to pushy."

"She's strong willed—a lot like my mother. Maybe that is why I love her so much. But, I really do hope the two of you become better acquainted. Maybe become friends."

"Well, I'll try. But, that 'you have to do things my way' attitude is going to be a little hard to take. I don't react well to that. I'll find my own dress for the wedding and I'm not wearing something I don't like just because she designed it."

"Okay Mom, I'm not arguing about what you wear to the wedding. I just want to make sure you're there and have a good time. You know we've made hotel reservations for the wedding party for the night before and the night after."

"That's what Victoria said. Jon, I wanted to mention something—and please don't get mad—but do you have a pre-nuptial agreement drawn up? I mean, to protect the corporation. I know nothing will happen to the marriage, but just in case."

"Yes, Mom. One of the partners who practices family law drew it up. I haven't presented it to Victoria yet, but I plan to do that this weekend."

"Okay, good. I just wanted to be sure. I know as a lawyer you always think of these things, but we hadn't discussed it."

"By the way, I checked out Mike Fitzgerald and found he has a record. Just petty stuff, he doesn't seem smart enough to do anything major, but I wanted to let you know I was on top of it."

"Thanks, I don't know what I'd do without you. I'm sure the Corpus Christi Police are working on it, but I haven't heard from them."

"Well, I hope they are," Jon replied.

"Oh, I almost forgot, did you get the name of the wedding planner? They need to know how many to plan for with hotel accommodations, etc. I'll make sure you get her card and you can call her with your number. Do you plan to bring Alex, and does he need a room of his own?"

"Jon!"

"Mom, he said he spent the night and I don't think

it was on the couch. I am not judging, I just need to know a head count for the wedding."

"I don't know, I haven't talked to him about it yet."

"Well, I'll send you the card and you can let the planner know. I gotta' go. I love you," he said and clicked the phone off.

Meg said she loved him too, but doubted he heard her before hanging up.

Alex's baseball cap was becoming evident over the top of the sand dunes as he walked toward the garden and she waved. He waved back, smiling.

"Hey, Sam." Alex strolled comfortably up to the chef with one hand behind him. "Nice tomatoes today."

"Every day." Sam smiled while filling his wagon with produce.

"Morning, Lady." Alex reached out and took Meg's hand, placing a quick peck on her cheek.

It was surprising how comfortable they were with each other. Meg would have normally run from such intimacy, but it just seemed ordinary for them.

"Good morning, Alex." Meg smiled at the man holding her hand.

He handed her a small sunflower that he had picked on the way through the garden.

"How sweet! I'll put it in water."

Sam pulled the wagon to the back door and reached in his pocket to pay for the produce. "That reminds me," he said, pointing to the sunflower, "we need centerpieces for tonight. I have some scissors, may I help myself?"

"Of course. The lavender is ready and there are always sunflowers and sea oats. Take all you want. They're trying to take over."

Sam walked to the back of the garden.

"I think I'll attend my son's wedding after all." Meg turned to Alex. "I thought at first I wouldn't with all that has gone on. I just didn't want to go into Corpus Christi and deal with people. But, I've changed my mind. Jon is my only child and I need to be there to support him. I was wondering if you would like to escort me. Jon and Victoria have both asked if you were coming. They have room reservations for the night of the rehearsal dinner and the night after the wedding. It will be extravagant I'm sure, but might be fun. What do you say, want to go?"

"I'm honored to be your escort and would love to attend," Alex said without hesitation. "But, I didn't bring much with me and have no formal clothes. I'd need to go shopping."

"Funny you should mention that, because I need to shop too and was going to ask if you could take me into Corpus Christi. We could shop and have dinner somewhere—my treat, of course. I just don't want to do it on my own."

"I can pay my own way. I've been selling a few paintings and besides, I need to visit the gallery where my latest art is being held captive. When do you want to go?"

"Well, I just found out the wedding is being moved up, so I don't have as much time as I thought. There is a little boutique where I normally shop, and I could call them to let them know what I'm looking for and they could have a few things ready. Why don't you contact your gallery and see when a good time to visit will be, and then we'll work around that schedule."

"Meg, can I have all this lavender?" Sam called out

from the middle of the garden.

"You talk to Sam and I'll call the gallery." Alex pulled his phone from the pocket of his jeans and waved her away.

Meg walked up the hill to the lavender where Sam was loading his wagon. "Here, let me get you something to put them in. Here is a coffee can." She took the lavender from the chef, placing it in the rusted and used coffee can.

"I have a wonderful lavender cherry sauce for pound cake or ice cream, and I could use them in the centerpieces too. You need to come by and try it." He waved goodbye and began his journey back to the restaurant, pulling the cart behind him.

"I just talked to the gallery," Alex said, walking up behind her. "What about tomorrow?"

"That would be wonderful. Maybe we could eat at Le Chez's tonight? Sam keeps asking when we're coming."

"Sounds great, I'll call for reservations." Alex pulled his cell phone from his pocket again and dialed the number that had become familiar to him of late.

****

The scent of seafood filled the air as Alex opened the door for Meg. The cool intimate restaurant was filled with vacationers and the occasional local diner. Meg looked around the room for a familiar face when Sam came from the back, wiping sweat from his forehead. He ran a tight ship with the few employees he had. He did all the cooking. There were only two waiters, a busboy, and a young local girl working the front door as a hostess. Currently, she was in the corner flirting with the busboy as the door opened, and never looked up.

"Rachelle, customers," Sam said with a quiet intensity and then walked quickly to greet Meg and Alex himself.

"My friends! Finally, you have come to let me cook for you. Meg." He kissed her cheek. "And Alex." He extended his hand and shook Alex's firmly. "Meg, you won't believe the lavender-cherry sauce I made from your garden. Be sure to save room for dessert. But, first let me start you off with my famous blackberry martini. It is a specialty of the house. Rachelle will seat you and I'll get you started with some appetizers."

Meg and Alex were quickly ushered to the table that faced the water. She was sure that the best table had been saved for them. The darkened restaurant overlooked the strand of water between the mainland and the tiny island. The sun was setting behind clouds and threw off a pink and orange glow to everything around it.

The waiter quickly brought dark martinis with a twist of lemon on the edge of the sugar coated glass and a plate of raw veggies with hummus. Meg knew she could make a meal off the appetizers and determined to pace herself. She was starving after the day working in the garden. The tartness of the martini surprised her and she savored the taste on her tongue before letting it slide down her throat.

"Great hummus," Alex said as he dipped the cucumber and scooped up the mashed chickpeas and garlic. He smiled at her over the candle in the middle of the table. "This is wonderful. We should have done this earlier. What took us so long to get here?"

"I don't know. We've both been busy."

"You should never get too busy to have a nice dinner with friends."

"You're right. We'll plan more time for dinner at Le Chez."

They never saw a menu even though the specials were on a blackboard when they first entered the restaurant. She wasn't offered a choice of items and the entre was served before Meg could fill up on appetizers. Sam had sent out his best Shrimp Scampi piled on top of a mound of homemade linguine pasta with a bottle of Chardonnay, warm garlic rolls, and butter. Before she could get too full, Meg pushed the plate of scampi aside. Alex refilled her wine glass and the sun made one final attempt before setting for the evening.

"Let me get you a box for that," the waiter said as he took the plate and replaced it with a slice of pound cake with a cherry sauce over the top. From his tray he produced coffee and asked if she took sugar or cream. Meg knew she had to try the dessert even though she felt she might burst and she would take home the leftovers for later.

She looked at Alex and they both tried to hide the smile that said "I can't eat another thing." And they dove into the dessert. The buttery pound cake was moist without the sauce but the cherries had a hint of lavender to set it off so that it was spectacular. The scent of the lavender hit her nose first, and Meg wondered if she tasted or smelled the herb in the sauce. It was hard to tell.

Finally looking up from the dessert, Meg realized they were almost alone in the diner, when Sam emerged from the kitchen with a glass of wine in his hand. He pulled a chair up to the table and sat down with a plop.

"Well, tell me it was wonderful!" he said with a gleam in his eye.

"Oh, it was wonderful." Alex patted his stomach and Meg agreed.

"Wonderful. But, too much. I have to take this home too. I can't eat here too often or I'll be huge."

"Oh, like you have to worry about that." Sam smiled. "I hope you liked the wine pairing. It is my favorite." He held his glass up to the candlelight and swirled it around then tasted it. "I'm so happy you came for dinner. I want you to come back on Friday when we have lobster. I make a drawn butter with a hint of rosemary. I think you will love it."

Meg heard the last patron leave and the doors shut. They were the only guests in the place. "Sam, we didn't mean to keep you so late." She stood and the men followed her lead.

"Yes," Alex said, "get us a bill and we'll be out of your hair."

"Nonsense, there is no bill for my friends. I've been expecting you for some time. Besides, I invited you."

"No, really, we planned to pay for dinner."

"No, your money's no good here. Besides, all the flavors come from your garden. Kyle, can you get these folks their boxes and we'll let them leave?" Sam signaled the waiter as Meg and Alex prepared to leave.

"Thank you for a wonderful dinner, Sam." Meg was kissed on both cheeks and ushered out the door.

"Just come back soon," Sam replied as Kyle handed Alex the box of food she was unable to eat. Meg knew it would still be wonderful tomorrow.

They walked hand in hand in the moonlight toward the other shore of the island and Meg's beach house, breathing the night air and listening to sounds of the waves rushing up on the beach. A perfect ending to a perfect evening, and one that Meg hoped to repeat many more times.

Chapter 25

"I can't believe he's done this to me!" Victoria stomped around the room with a sheaf of papers in her hand. Fitzgerald still lay on the bed partially covered with a sheet. Their lovemaking today had been rough and tumultuous. Victoria was in a mean mood and it showed in her intimacy. Not that she was ever very intimate. Sex with her was more of a contest to see who was in charge. That was fine with Fitzgerald. He could do rough, but it was rougher than normal. It was obvious that her head was not in the game.

"If you're not happy with the numbers then get the man in bed and change his mind," Fitzgerald replied. "That shouldn't be a problem for you."

"I mean a pre-nup? Really? Who does he think he's dealing with?"

"He's a lawyer—he wants it all tied up in a pretty bow. Besides, in today's world everyone with money signs a pre-nup. Like I said, just get him to change the numbers. Change the amount, and change the length of time that you have to stay married to get it. Shouldn't be a problem. Of course the first draft will be to his advantage. He probably expected a negotiation."

"Well, he's gonna' get one!"

"Just stay calm and remember who's in charge. He should think it's his idea, not yours."

She fingered the engagement ring on her finger: a

full two carats of clear, perfect diamond solitaire in the center with baguettes on each side. "Maybe the ring," she said. "I could say it is too much and I didn't need such extravagance. We could return it for something smaller and simpler—use the proceeds for charity. That's it. A good way to get into his heart, and then maybe we could do away with the honeymoon in Paris, if that is what it takes. I'd much rather get more money at the end of this marriage than at the beginning. Besides, it rains in Paris."

"It rains in Corpus Christi," Fitzgerald replied, yawning.

"Don't argue with me!" She pulled the dress over her head and slipped into her pumps. "I've got a client." She walked out the door with her bag hanging on her arm without even a goodbye.

Fitzgerald rolled over and pulled the covers over his head. It was time he paid another visit to Ms. Stanford and began their negotiations. He knew once Victoria was married, he wouldn't be needed anymore—not that he was now.

****

Alex's thoughts were distracted remembering the meeting at Meg's house the morning Jon found him there. He tried to paint, but his heart wasn't in it. It must have been difficult for Jon to see his mother and think of her as a sexual being with a boyfriend. After all, Jon was right about the strange things happening to Meg after meeting Alex. He wasn't the reason for the blackmail—he just came into the scene about the same time. But still, if Alex had been in Jon's shoes, would he have felt any different? Maybe he should pay a visit to Jon's office and see if he could smooth things over.

Meg was important to him.

He was afraid if he called to get an appointment he might never get in, so he cleaned his brushes, got in the van, and left the island without saying a word to anyone. He had to make things right if he could. Besides, he lied on the application for the grant, and he was sure Jon had guessed that by now. He'd offer again to pay the money back if it would help.

After finding directions to the high-rise office building in downtown Corpus Christi, he opened the door and took the elevator to the fifteenth floor. It opened to a huge entry with a reception desk at the front where an attractive woman sat behind the desk. Alex immediately felt ill at ease in his jeans and sandals. He was suddenly aware of the fact that he still had paint on his hands. He could have at least cleaned up a little, but didn't think of it in his rush to get out the door.

"May I help you?" the receptionist asked when he walked up to the desk.

"Yes, I'm Alex Wallace and I'd like to see Jon Stanford if he is in."

"Mr. Stanford is in court, but is expected back soon. Do you have an appointment?"

"No, I don't have an appointment, but I am a friend of his mother's and I was hoping to get to talk to him for just a few moments. It won't take long."

"If you will have a seat, I'll see if his assistant can work you in." She reached for the phone.

Alex walked across the room and sat in one of the overstuffed chairs next to a mahogany table and picked up a magazine. He began to thumb through the periodical when a young woman walked out the door toward him.

"Mr. Wallace?" she said as she approached.

"Yes." He placed the magazine back down on the table and stood.

"I'm Joan, Mr. Stanford's assistant. He's due back from court soon and I am sure he will want to see you. Is Meg okay?"

"Yes, Meg is fine. I didn't mean to alarm you. She doesn't even know I'm here. I just wanted to talk to Jon for a moment about a personal matter if he has time."

"Of course. I'll see if I can work you in. He has some time between appointments." She walked back behind the paneled doors.

Within moments she reemerged with coffee in her hands in a china cup and saucer with the firm's logo on the side. "I didn't ask if you wanted something to drink. I hope you take it black. Mr. Stanford will see you know."

Alex stepped into the oversized office with an ornate rug on the floor. Jon's office held antique law books in an equally old lawyer's cabinet on one wall. They were a reminder of the past before legal research was done online. Jon sat behind a large desk with a view of the city from a floor-to-ceiling window. His arms crossed over his chest, he eyed Alex warily when he walked in and didn't stand to welcome him into the office.

"Alex," he said, leaning forward and gesturing to the chair in front of the desk. "Joan says you want to talk to me, and nothing's wrong with Mom."

"That's right. I thought you and I needed to talk. Thank you for taking the time to meet with me."

"Anything for a friend of Mom's." Jon didn't even

crack a smile.

"That's part of what I want to talk to you about." Alex looked for a place to set the saucer and was offered no help. "I'm sure it was a shock finding me at your Mom's house the other day."

Jon cleared his throat and shuffled in his seat.

"First of all, I want you to know, I have nothing but the best intentions toward your mother. She's a wonderful woman. We became friends because we were next to each other every day with my paintings and her vegetable stand. But, the feelings have grown between us. I know she feels the same. We're not kids. We've both lived alone a long time, and I think we like being together. We're both tired of being by ourselves."

Jon stared at Alex without moving.

"But, that is not the only thing I am here to talk to you about."

"No?" Jon asked, raising his eyebrows.

"No, I also want to talk about the grant."

"You mean the one to Alex Simmons?"

"Yes, that's the one. My name is legally Simmons. It was never changed when my Mom married. But, I had always used Wallace, her married name, at her insistence when I was young. I used Simmons so I could apply for the grant without the trial coming up in a background check. The records were sealed, you know that already, but I was afraid that they could be unsealed if the right person came along. I was right. You got them unsealed."

Jon didn't react.

"Yeah," Jon said after a long silence, "we didn't find much under Alex Simmons and you were lucky. There weren't many applicants that year, or you probably wouldn't have gotten the grant."

"Well, you know by reading the documents that I was exonerated. I didn't attack that young woman. Nothing could be further from the truth. She was the one that harassed me. Men don't like to admit to that kind of thing, but it does happen. She was a student. I wouldn't sleep with a student. When she didn't get what she wanted, she invented the story to get back at me. She accused me of attempted rape, and I landed in court. After the courts found me innocent, I lost my job because the school didn't want the story to get out about an accused professor still on the payroll. Well, that and the fact that her father was on the board of regents didn't help either."

Jon sat silent, looking at Alex from across the desk. Neither man looked away. "You're in love with my mother?" Jon asked, speaking first.

"Yes." He paused. "We've really not talked about that. I mean, I haven't said that out loud before, but yes, I love your mother. She is a wonderful woman. She has had a hard life, and I'd like to think I could help soften it a little for her. I'd like to be there to protect and take care of her a little. It's obvious that she has always been the one that took care of everything. She probably needs a rest."

"That's true. However, if you can get her to let go of the reins a little you'd be lucky. She's a very strong-willed woman. But, I'll bet you've noticed that."

Alex laughed. "Don't I know it! I almost never got her to let me help with the rabbit problem. What ever happened to that guy?"

"I don't know. I haven't heard much about him lately."

"Well, Jon, I wanted to lay my cards on the table. I can imagine how much you want to take care of your mother and how concerned you are for her. But, about the grant, I can pay that money back a little at a time if you want. I'm selling some paintings and since I was less than forthcoming about the name, I wouldn't blame you at all if you wanted the money back."

"The Stanford Corporation is solvent; we don't need the money back."

"Of course, I didn't mean you needed the money back. But still, I can pay you back."

"No, that won't be necessary." Jon fingered the gold pen that lay on his desk. "But, I would like to see your paintings. I assume you painted the new one in Mom's kitchen, the woman in the sunhat?"

"Yes. I painted it from memory and of course you can't see Meg's face, but I wanted to commemorate her meeting with the rabbit. It was what brought us together. Please come by the gallery any time. I'd love to show you what I'm working on. I have a new medium using the juice from the produce in your mom's garden."

"Really? You are painting with juice?"

"It has really been great. It was an accident the first time I did it, and the colors were so wonderful, I haven't used paint since."

Joan stepped in the door, pointing to her watch.

"Well, if you will excuse me, I have an appointment. I promise to come by the gallery soon."

"Certainly." Alex stood, extending his paint-stained hand. Jon clasped it and escorted him to the door. Jon was a lot like his mother after all, and this thought made Alex smile as he left the office.

Chapter 26

Alex drove through the city of Corpus Christi as Meg directed him. He seemed unsure of the big city traffic. She led him to the boutique that she knew and once loved. Parking the van across the street, she held his hand as they crossed to the store.

Inside, the bell tinkled as the door closed behind them. The smells and sounds brought back memories to Meg she hadn't thought of in years, not all of them good. With her hair styled and makeup on, she had worn the yellow sheath again. It had become her "going to the city" dress and she decided to wear it once more. Maybe she should buy more than one outfit to wear for the wedding—something for the rehearsal dinner and then something to travel back and forth in. Something she wouldn't wear in the garden.

A quick young woman with sparkling red hair stepped from the door behind the counter. "Ms. Stanford!" She ran to grab her hands and kiss her cheek. "It's been so long. We thought you had forgotten us! I hope you liked what we picked out for your dinner engagement."

"Anna, it is a pleasure to see you again. Yes, the outfits were lovely. This is my friend Alex Wallace and we're here to find something for my son's wedding."

"Yes, that's what you said—purples, I believe you mentioned. I've set aside several things. I didn't have a lot of time, but if you find something else that isn't in your size, we can make a rush order. Now if you'll step this way, I have some things hung up for you next to the dressing room. Mr. Wallace, if you would like to have a seat, Kristen will get you anything you like to eat or drink. You know it takes a woman a while to make up her mind."

Kristen was tall and thin with severely short black hair—in deep contrast to the loads of red curls that Anna wore. Each woman looked like she just stepped from the pages of a fashion magazine with the latest hair, makeup, and manicure styles. Kristen's deep blue nails matched her dress and the Cleopatra-style eyeliner set off her overly green eyes. She must have been wearing colored contacts. She smiled and showed perfect teeth—probably capped.

"Mr. Wallace, I have some wonderful Mimosas in the back, or the coffee is on. We also have bottled water and soft drinks. I could also scare up a beer if you would like. What is your pleasure?"

Alex smiled. They spared no expense. "Coffee would be great, Kristen," he said and winked at Meg as she was led away to the treasure trove of styles picked out especially for her.

Meg found a long flowing dress in plum with sequins and a sheer jacket that could be taken off if the weather was warm. Anna even thought of shoes in a sling back with low heels. She knew Meg well enough not to offer accessories other than an evening bag. Meg had her own jewelry, thanks to her mother, and it was much nicer than anything in the boutique. Mrs. Stanford never wore costume jewelry.

A pale pink ensemble was chosen for the rehearsal

dinner and then capris for the rest of the weekend—all with matching shoes and bags. Alex nodded his approval at her choices, and Meg smiled. She never needed anyone's approval, but found she was delighted that he liked the way she looked in the clothes.

With her bags securely in the van, they walked to the men's store close by. She had taken Jon there many times and she knew he still shopped there for the suits he wore to the office. Alex's tastes were simple and he quickly found a suit for the wedding, and sports coat and pants for the rehearsal dinner along with a couple of shirts. Like most men, he didn't take too long to shop.

"You know, I don't even have any dress shoes with me. I put a lot of things in storage when I left the university and came here. I guess I'll need shoes too." The salesman took his purchases to the front of the store.

"I can help you with that, sir," the salesman said and led him to a row of shoes in the back of the store. "We carry all the name brands."

"Well, comfort is the name of the game. Show me something comfortable that will still look good, and I prefer a loafer.

"I don't think I've spent this much money on clothes at one time ever!" Alex said as they left the store. "My style of shopping is to go to the clearance racks in the back, and only when I absolutely have to. At the university I wore jeans and turtlenecks most of the time, and I always had a tee shirt in the back if we were into clay or oil paints. I didn't stand at the front of a huge hall and lecture students. My classes were more hands on. But, these are nice." He pointed to the suit bag he had slung over his shoulder. "And more to the point, this has been a wonderful day with you. Like most men, shopping is not my thing, unless there is a beautiful woman on my arm." He smiled.

"You're so sweet. It has been a lovely day." He kissed her lightly on the lips. "But, we need to go to your gallery," Meg said. "It's near La Retama Park, right? I think there is some construction going on Chaparral Street so we might have to wind our way around some, but we'll find it. And there are some delightful bistros and things along the way. We could get a bite to eat afterward, if you would like."

The gallery was open when they arrived and the owner was in the back. Tom Matthews stepped from the store room and approached Alex and Meg as they looked at the paintings on the wall.

"That's a nice one—painted by a local artist," he began. "Alex! I didn't recognize you without the baseball cap." He walked toward them, hand outstretched. He shook Alex's hand and reached for Meg's. "Mrs. Wallace?" Meg's face suddenly felt warm.

"No, Tom, this is my friend Meg. She lives on the island too. In fact she is the inspiration for my work— she and her garden. She grows the produce that I use as the medium."

"Meg," Tom said, "it is a pleasure to meet you, and I am so glad you've inspired Alex in his work. We love what he has done here and want more! I had a customer in here yesterday who wanted to buy the only "Wallace" I had. But, I said there were more on the way. I hope that is true."

"You bet. I have several in the van with me."

"Well, let's go get them." Tom said, heading for the door.

Meg watched the men walking to the van and marveled at how easily Alex interacted with everyone he met—unlike her. All she did was blush when she was called Mrs. Wallace. Anyway, would that be so bad? Alex was a wonderful man, and changing her name from Stanford could be a blessing in disguise. But, marriage after all these years seemed like an alien idea. She was happy like she was, wasn't she? Besides, it wasn't like they had discussed it. They really weren't a couple, were they?

"So, Meg, you are really Alex's inspiration, huh?" Tom asked when the paintings were leaning up against the wall.

"Well, so he says. He does use my produce for the medium and even though he came to Sandhill Island to paint the sea, he loves the little beach house I live in. He's painted the landscape there before. But, I really doubt that he needs much outside inspiration."

"Well, Alex, your paintings are inspired, wherever it comes from. Now the juice that you paint with—for want of a better word—will it fade?"

"It's been sealed and should last for years like watercolor."

"I'll call the buyer this afternoon and let him know these are here. I can almost guarantee your first sale. And I'd like to have a show soon of just your work. Can we plan on that?"

Alex looked at Meg and then back at Tom. "You mean only this medium, or other things as well?"

"Whatever you have that you would like to sell; we'll put it all in here. I'll take care of the advertising and it would be nice if we could do it during one of the First Friday Art Walks—they bring in a lot of people. We have them on the first Friday of every month and they bring out the regulars, and a lot of other people that normally don't come out. We could feature your work."

"That would be great. Let me know when to deliver the rest of the work."

"Anytime would be great. Would it be okay to prepare for next month?"

Alex nodded, smiling.

Meg was sure his work would be widely recognized soon. Once outside the gallery, she grabbed his hand. "Alex, I'm so excited for you!" She kissed his cheek. "And I'm starving. Let's celebrate and find something to eat." They walked hand-in-hand down the street after they left the gallery. There were eclectic little restaurants all along the area with galleries and boutiques—but one with a turquoise door caught her eye. "How about here for some dinner?" She pulled him in the door.

Inside, the air was full of Italian spices and yeast bread baking. Checked tablecloths covered the tiny square tables, and empty wine bottles held candles in the middle. It looked like you were in the heart of Tuscany, not on the seashore of Texas.

Looking at the menus, Meg tried to decide on pasta or pizza—or maybe a meatball sandwich. Everything looked fabulous, but in the end it was her nose that made the decision for her. "What about the pizza?" she asked, "want to share a pizza and a bottle of wine?"

"I don't think anything else will do. I'm not going to even think about being healthy today. Deep dish?"

"Deep dish it is."

After the cold crisp salads and bread that came with the wine, Meg expected to be too full to eat the pizza, but she was wrong. Alex laughed as she tried to pull the stringy cheese from the pie and reached across the table to wipe tomato sauce off her chin.

"Oh, this is wonderful. The pizza, the wine, the day, but mostly you—I love you, Meg." He said it easily and with a sparkle in his eyes.

"That's just the wine talking." She smiled back around a bite of pizza.

He put the slice back on the plate, wiped his hands and reached across the table, picking up her finger that still dripped in sauce. "No, I mean it. I've thought of nothing else for some time. I love you, Meg. I love the way you make me feel young again, and I love just being with you, even if we're only drinking iced tea on my porch. I love you. I hope that doesn't run you off, but it needed to be said."

Meg looked into his warm gray eyes. "No. Surprisingly, it doesn't run me off. I haven't felt the way I feel in some time either. Maybe it was a long time coming, but I feel more comfortable with you than anyone in a long time. I think I may love you too."

"You think?"

"That sounded awful" she said, laughing quietly. "Let me try again. I have no idea how to have this conversation. I spent my life raising a son without his father. I was motherless as soon as she saw that I was pregnant, and was always an embarrassment to my father after her death. I know I've pushed more than one person away in my lifetime, but I'm tired of that. You have made me tired of that way of life. Yes, Alex,

I think I love you." She paused. "I really do. But, I still need a little time to be sure. Is that okay?" He smiled at her across the table. "What do you say to getting a to-go box and taking the pizza back to my house? If we hurry, we can still make the last ferry."

"Waiter," Alex called.

Strolling hand-in-hand through the garden in the moonlight, Alex and Meg, still giddy from the wine, giggled like teenagers as he ran his hands through her hair, kissing her lightly on the lips.

Alex carried the bags in the door and hung them on the doorknob in the living room, then opened the door to the front porch to look out.

"Tide's in." Meg looked out to sea. "Let's go wade a little before we go in." She pointed to the ocean and led him through the door and out to her front yard. This was why she lived by the ocean, its sights and smells intoxicated her.

The cool foam covered her bare feet as she walked into ankle deep water with Alex by the hand. Moonlight shone through the clouds. It had finally cooled off a little after the sun went down, and the humidity wasn't as oppressive.

His arm slid around her waist and he nuzzled her neck. They stood looking out at the lightly rolling sea they both loved like a child. A spoiled child sometimes—always getting its way, but still they loved it. What mysteries did its depths hold? What bounty could it give up if it was encouraged? What terrors would it inflict if you didn't respect it?

A cool current rolled in over their legs and feet and Meg relaxed. She turned to face Alex and kissed him passionately. The moon and the sea had been responsible for passion in so many ways since time began, and they were just another speck in time to them. But, it was their speck in time, and Meg and Alex were engulfed in the feelings brought on by nature.

Meg was suddenly hit from behind, knocking both of them down as the wave rolled over them and dragged them out into deeper water. She floundered and spit for a second and then sat up with water up to her chin. Alex began to laugh, reaching for her as the current threatened to pull her further out if she didn't stand up quickly. She knew better than to turn her back on the sea.

A crab scuttled away, making the sand under her feet move. She fell again. This time Alex was on his feet grabbing her hand, but another wave knocked them both down. Before she was pulled out even further, she stood and looked at the incoming waves washing their way.

"Come on!" she shouted. And the wind changed directions, blowing her voice away. They ran for the house, soaked to the bone.

Once inside the safety of the screened porch, he grabbed her, passionately kissing her neck and pulling at her clothes. She led him to the bedroom, and they shed their wet clothing along the way. The salty water leaked out of the fabric and pooled onto the old wooden floor. It could be cleaned up tomorrow.

Chapter 27

Fitzgerald tiptoed through the back door of the beach house. He wore a black ski mask and turtleneck for effect. He knew Meg would recognize him, but it might scare her even more at first. Surprisingly, he had to jimmy the latch this time. She must have decided to fix the lock after the last time he was here. Not that it slowed him down much. He could hear snoring in the bedroom that didn't sound female. The artist was probably back in her bed again.

Tiptoeing through the house, he peeked in the bedroom and could barely make out two lumps in the bed. His plan was to push her a little harder this time. Scare her a little by showing up in the middle of the night at her bedside. But, she was not alone and that changed things. Still, maybe he could scare her in some other way.

Walking past the kitchen table, he saw the antique silver sugar bowl. It looked out of place in the tumbledown house. It was obviously old and worth some money. He knew a guy that would pay top dollar for items like this. He picked it up and dumped the small amount of sugar in the bottom onto the table and pocketed it in his jacket, then walked out through the door that led to the garden. She would surely miss the bowl and know that someone had been in the house. Maybe that was enough to remind her she couldn't run from her past. She was getting to be a problem. And if she wouldn't pay, maybe it would be better to get rid of her than to blackmail her.

Back out in the garden the wind had changed directions and blew in off the water from the south. Hurricane season was coming, and some of the old timers said it was going to be a bad one this year. The moon was full and the tide was higher than normal. It wouldn't be full again for another month. But, the storms were supposed to start in the next few days. That meant the tide would be lower when they hit and would make flooding less of a possibility.

****

Meg woke earlier than usual that morning and found that Alex was already gone. As she walked through the kitchen she stopped, staring at the place where her mother's sugar bowl normally sat on the table. She couldn't remember where she put it. She'd looked everywhere in the small house and knew she hadn't moved it. Had someone been in her house again? Why didn't she feel safe in her own home anymore? She came to the island to get away from the world—and it found her anyway. Maybe Alex could help her look for the silver heirloom.

On top of that, the weather didn't feel right. The ever-present humidity felt heavier than normal, and the sea breeze had died down. The locals were talking about hurricane season again like it was a visitor to be endured. One that wouldn't go away. Paul, the shrimper, said his niece was with the weather detachment at Keesler Air Force Base and she had warned him of the possible bad weather just last night. She had grown up on the island, and though it had never taken a direct hit from a big hurricane, she worried about her family. Meg wondered if Paul just liked to brag about his niece, but it was always good to hear from an expert.

Alex kept mentioning boarding up her windows, but that would mean she would have to leave and she wasn't ready. Instead, he pulled all the plywood out of the shed and placed it under the windows in preparation. That way it would go faster when the time came. She hoped he was wrong about having to hang the plywood. In the few years that she had lived in the tiny house, the storms had never been bad enough to be called a hurricane.

She pulled her cart to the produce stand with the darkest, ripest veggies on top saved for Alex and his paintings. Next year she would try some heirloom tomatoes in greens and plum colors. Maybe some beets too. Alex would probably like them and Sam also.

Alex's paintings were selling before he could even get them on canvas these days. The gallery constantly called wanting more, and he had a show coming up. He was secretly keeping the best ones in the back away from prying eyes so he could make a splash at the First Friday Art Walks at La Retama Park. He was becoming a hit, at least locally, and if Tom Matthews had anything to say about it, he would take him global. Meg couldn't be happier for Alex. But, she was unsure that he felt the same. He said fame and fortune were never what he wanted. Meg understood wanting privacy so she didn't push him, but she did introduce him to her accountant. At this rate, he would eventually need some help.

Most nights he stayed at his place so he could work

late. She didn't mind. She needed her time alone too, but on the nights he came over, she made a nice dinner, opened a bottle of wine, and they relaxed into the evening. It was becoming increasingly evident that they were an item, as Jon would say. They had both said they loved each other, so that had to count for something, right? Meg didn't know how these things were supposed to work, but she knew in her heart that now that she had met him, she didn't want to live without him, even though she wasn't good at expressing her feelings.

At the produce stand she began to unload the vegetables, flowers, and herbs she had carefully stacked in her cart, when the door to the art studio next door opened.

"Good morning, you're early." Alex had a sleepy smile and a cup of coffee in one hand.

"I am a little early." Meg smiled in return. "The weather woke me up. It is so still and humid it's almost hard to breathe. I saved you the best of the best. They're over there." She gestured to the back of the lot. "Any more of that coffee?"

"Yes, and I was thinking it might need some ice this morning, what do you think?"

"Sounds great," Meg said.

"Here comes your favorite chef." Alex pointed with his coffee cup to the overweight man panting as he jiggled their way down the street. "I'd better get my stuff first." Alex picked up his painting medium before the chef made a salad out of it, and took it into the gallery.

Meg smiled. Sam Taylor from Le Chez waddled down the street to get the first chance at her produce.

She brought them to him this morning before he had a chance to pick them himself. She hoped he would approve of what she picked.

"Good morning, Alex, Meg." He gasped as he trotted to the produce stand. "Whew, it is so hot! Or maybe it is the humidity. Anyway, it's miserable. Some of the fishermen were talking about hurricane weather at dinner last night. What do you think?"

"Well, the weather is certainly changing and seems unsettled. You need some produce today? I have some great basil too." She pointed to the coffee can full of the fresh cut herbs. "I picked a little earlier today."

"I'm thinking cold salads—lots of cold food today and maybe an antipasto platter with jugs of iced tea and Sangria."

"Sounds wonderful," Meg said, smiling.

"Why don't you and Alex join us for dinner tonight? My treat."

"That's so sweet, Sam. Let me talk to Alex."

Sam stepped in front of her and touched her arm. "Meg, just let me say how nice it is to see you with someone. You deserve it. He's a great guy and I think it's time you were no longer alone. Just my opinion, but you make a cute couple."

The word couple surprised Meg. Of course they enjoyed each other's company and she knew he loved her—but couple was a permanent kind of word. And she thought she liked it. "He's great," she said a little shyly.

"Okay, give me what you've got. I'll find something to do with all of it. Don't unload it; let's just pull it to the back door of the restaurant and I'll pay you there."

Meg walked down the street with Sam and they talked casually as Alex watched from the front door of his shop. She was aware that she had changed in the last few months, since he first met her. She felt more open, and made more friends all the time.

When she pulled the empty wagon back to her stand, Alex was in his usual spot with two iced coffees waiting on her arrival. In the window was a poster for the First Friday Art Walks at La Retama Park.

"You're not working?" she asked.

"I'm taking a break and watching the most beautiful woman in the world walk down the street." Alex smiled.

"Oh, now you're just exaggerating." She leaned down to kiss him. It struck her that she had never done anything like that in public before, and she liked it. She wanted people to know that she and Alex were a couple.

"No, never," he replied, taking her hand and kissing it. "Will you go to the Art Walk with me tomorrow? Maybe you could get the chef to pick his own veggies and we could make a day of it."

"I could probably do that. By the way, Sam asked us to join him for dinner tonight. Do you have time?"

He stood and pulled her inside the shop. "That sounds good. Let me show you what I have ready, and you tell me what you like." He led her to the back of the studio that doubled as an apartment.

They walked past the pastel paintings on easels in the front of the shop to the larger room behind. It was a combination kitchen and bedroom with a closet in the middle. The room was full of paintings leaning against the walls. Several sizes were finished, and most included her beach house or the shore it sat on. He had branched out to include the harbor in a few of the paintings, with pelicans sitting on posts poking out of the deep green water. Foam floated on still water, and wild waves flowed through others. The sun was setting in the haze in one painting, but most included a sunrise when the air was clean and clear. And sweet light from the evening before sunset caught the sunrays off the water that sparkled like diamonds in another. She had never seen such passion in a painting, and they were all painted with the juice from her produce. How he managed the colors was beyond her.

"Alex, these are wonderful!" Meg exclaimed as she hugged him. "Really, wonderful."

He turned her to face him and held her head in his hands. "That means the world to me—the fact that the most important person in my life likes my work." He kissed her deeply on the lips.

"No, not like, I love them," she said when she had caught her breath.

The bell to the shop rang and the sound of footsteps echoed across the wooden floor.

"Anyone home?" called a familiar voice.

"Jon!" Meg exclaimed as she pulled away from Alex. "How did you know where to find me?" She walked back to the front of the store.

"Oh, just an inkling." He smiled at his mother and walked into the room.

He wrapped her in a warm embrace and then extended a hand to Alex. His face changed only slightly as he shook the hand of his mother's lover. Meg knew he was still unsure of Alex, but he was warming up to the idea. Maybe.

"Alex, good to see you." He looked around the room. "Nice paintings."

"Oh, these are nothing, you should see what is going to the art festival in Corpus tomorrow," Meg said.

"Nice to see you too, Jon." Alex shook his hand. There was a noticeable change in their attitudes since the morning in Meg's kitchen. Alex gestured to the back room to show Jon the latest paintings.

"Great little art studio." Jon looked around as he walked to the back room. Then he stopped as he entered the kitchen/bedroom cluttered with paintings leaning against the wall in every nook and cranny. The paintings of the ocean he knew so well were lined up in every conceivable manner on the floor, on the table, and one even lay on the bed. "But, you're running out of room."

"Your mom and I are loading these up early tomorrow and heading for Corpus. So, they won't be here much longer."

"He has a one-artist-show at the gallery and my money says they'll all sell." Meg smiled with pride.

Jon walked to the one that lay on the bed. It was his mother's bungalow from a view in the garden. Looking down the side of the dilapidated house with one shutter askew, the view was a rising sea with dark thunderclouds in the background. "How much? Can I buy this one before it goes to market?"

"It's yours." Alex did not name a price.

"No, I want to buy it. I'm not looking for a handout. But, I'd like to hang it in my office."

"I'm sure you don't need a handout. But it needs a frame. None of these are framed until the buyer tells me what they want. I think it's good to give them the opportunity to frame them with their decor. Some artists frame them to go with the painting, and that is a good idea too, but I want the buyer to have a say in the framing. Tom Matthews has a framer that he likes to use and he does wonderful work."

"You have it framed as you think it needs to be, and I'll come by the studio tomorrow in Corpus and pay you. Just don't let it get away." Then Jon turned to face Meg.

"Mom, any more trouble with notes from people trying to blackmail you? I talked to the detectives in Corpus Christi yesterday and they seem to have your case on the back burner. I guess if there isn't a double homicide, they aren't interested."

"I haven't heard any more. Maybe he got bored and went away. However, I couldn't find your grandmother's sugar bowl this morning. I don't know, maybe I just misplaced it. I don't think anyone has been in the house. But, you didn't come all the way out here just to ask me that. What's up?"

"Keep looking, it's probably somewhere in the house. But, there is one little thing. Victoria has changed her mind again about the wedding. She just wants a civil ceremony at the Courthouse. I know a judge that will perform the ceremony, and I hope you will still come. It may be in a couple of days."

Meg's mind began to whirl. What girl didn't want a big wedding? Especially when she could design all the dresses herself and money was no object? "What changed her mind? I mean, I thought she and her family wanted to have a grand event at the country club."

"Well, she has decided that the money we were

going to spend could be better spent if given to charity. She's like that. I gave her the pre-nup and she didn't even flinch."

"She knows of course that most of our money goes to charity? I mean... maybe I'm over-thinking this, but it seems odd to me."

Jon's face began to darken and then abruptly stopped. He leaned down and kissed his mother on the forehead. "You're always seeing ghosts in the woodwork. She is just frugal, that's all, and it's something you should identify with. I'll let you know when we get the details worked out."

"Alex, don't let that painting get away tomorrow. Mark it sold and hang it on the wall, but it's mine." Then he turned and left.

"Do you think that's strange?" Meg said to Alex after Jon left. "I mean she keeps changing her mind about the wedding and moving it up."

"I think it would be better if I didn't get involved."

"I'm going to have someone check up on that young lady. Something about her bothers me."

Chapter 28

He walked down the street with his hat down low over his eyes, watching the people come and go through the art festival. Mike Fitzgerald knew the gallery was a few blocks down, but he wanted to get a feel about the people at the gathering. Mostly families, mothers with strollers, kids running this way and that hyped up on sugar, some serious art buyers—and then the vendors. The heat was oppressive and almost everyone was drinking water from a plastic bottle even though they were sweating it out faster than they could take it in. His shirt clung to him like a warm plastic wrapper to sticky candy. He had lived in this climate all his life and he understood humidity, but something was different. The atmosphere felt as unsettled as he did.

He saw the man through the window, sitting at the bar with a beer in his hand. He said he would be at the little bar on Water Street. It was ten o'clock in the morning and most people hadn't started drinking yet. But Robert Chung could always use a cold one.

****

Robert Chung—Bob to his buddies if he had any—downed another beer at the local watering hole. Sandhill Island. Did he really want to go back to that hell hole again for a few measly dollars? The guy had to come up with more if he wanted the job done this time. He killed the fisherman and now he was supposed to go after the fisherman's lover? After all, she was a woman, and not a young one at that. It wasn't like she would be much of a challenge, but he had a few scruples. He didn't like killing women or children. But, he was broke and five thousand dollars was more than he had in his bank account now.

He swirled the golden liquid in the bottom of the glass and then drained it. He could get more—at least double that. Ten thousand for a life seemed like a small amount when you thought about it. But, the guy said all he had was five. Maybe he could work out a double cross and blackmail the woman. She was the one with the money, right? The Stanfords always had money— hell they owned the whole damned island, so ten thousand was nothing to them. He would demand the five thousand up front from the guy, and another five when it was done. Then he could kidnap the woman instead of killing her. The son would pay the money he asked for. He had millions, not thousands. That would be enough for him to live on the rest of his life and he wouldn't have to worry anymore. He'd just take off for some little South American country and hide out. How hard could it be?

"Gimme another, Mack," he told the bartender.

And the bartender did as he was told. Once Bob got started, he seldom quit until someone carried him out. Just another day for Bob Chung. But, this time he would stay sober until the job was done. He had to.

****

Fitzgerald walked into the artificially cool and dark pub and casually walked past the guy at the bar, catching his eye. He moved to the table in the corner away from the windows and sat facing the man.

Fitzgerald watched as he drained his glass then slowly got up and walked to the bathroom, emerging a few minutes later bypassing the bar and sauntering to the table.

Eventually, after changing the channel on the TV to something more interesting, the bartender walked over and stood next to the table. "You guys buying this morning, or just takin' up room?" he asked.

"I'll take another," said Chung.

"Just water." Fitzgerald hoped this guy wasn't going to be trouble and could keep it together long enough to get the job done. He would get the negotiations out of the way soon, before he ended up with a huge bar tab.

"Five thousand was the agreed upon price," Fitzgerald said after the bartender left to refill Chung's ever-thirsty habit.

"Well, that's changed a little." Chung looked over Fitzgerald's shoulder at the TV. There was a map of the Gulf with a swirl of storms almost to Cuba. "It's five thousand now, and another five when the job is done."

"That's not what we agreed. Five thousand is all I can scrape together. It's five or nuthin'."

"Well, it's nuthin' then." Chung started to rise.

"Just hold on a second. We had a deal."

"Well, like I said, the deal has changed. Ten thousand..." he broke off as the beer arrived.

"You guys want to run a tab?" asked the bartender.

"Sure." Chung took a drink.

"No, I've got it." Fitzgerald reached for his wallet and threw the money on the table. "We won't be here that long."

The bartender grumbled something under his

breath as he shambled away.

"You know, I've been thinking, ten thousand isn't that much for a life, any life, especially one as rich as hers."

"I don't have it," Fitzgerald responded.

"So talk to that little piece of tail you run around with. She looks like she has money. Or does she not know about this?"

"Leave her out of it. This is between you and me."

"Well, I'd love to leave her out of it, but the deal has changed and if you want it done, you have to come up with the extra money."

Fitzgerald looked at the man across the table. His gray hair pulled back in a ponytail in need of washing and a three day old beard, he looked as rough as the job he said he could do. Maybe it was worth the extra money to have Meg out of the way and leaving only Jon to deal with when the time came. Then again, if the woman was dead and the extra money not paid, what was he going to do about it? Call the police? "All right, five up front and an additional five when the job is done. I know that she and the artist are here at the festival today at a gallery on Chaparral. His name is Alex Wallace and he is having a show at the gallery. Shouldn't be too hard to find."

"I think I can handle it." Chung took another swig.

Fitzgerald dug into his pocket and came up with a wad of cash, "Five thousand dollars, it's all there if you want to count it."

"I believe you. You wouldn't want to cheat me. That would be a bad mistake." He put the roll into his jacket pocket, finished the beer, and walked out the door toward Chaparral Street.

Chapter 29

Tom Mathews opened the door to the gallery and walked out. He could see Meg and Alex pulling up in the van.

"Did you bring me something wonderful?" He smiled, opening the door to the van for Meg.

"I hope so," Alex replied.

"Of course he did." Meg smiled and climbed out of the van, and then slid open the side door. The paintings lay stacked in the back, wrapped in sheets and assorted blankets to protect the precious cargo.

The early morning crowd was thickening like the humidity in the air as they strolled down the street. Local vendors were already set up with their wares and Meg wandered across the street while the men unloaded the van. Her eye was on a pottery stand that featured *raku* finishes—her favorite because they often came out of the kiln with blue and green iridescent colors like her beloved sea.

She picked up the lovely bowl, turning it over to see the artist's signature on the bottom, when the long black limo caught her eye. Jon was at the gallery to pick up his painting.

Placing the bowl back on the shelf, she raced across the street, almost running into a man with a long gray ponytail. He already smelled of stale beer, even though it was early in the morning.

"Excuse me." The man grabbed Meg's arms to steady her and smiled a wicked smile with stained yellow teeth.

"Of course." He let her go and she continued across the street. Jon stepped through the car door held open by the handsome chauffeur.

Greg, always smiling, tipped his hat to Meg as she hugged her son. "Mom," Jon said as he hugged her back. "Did Alex bring my painting?"

"Of course, it's inside. Go on in. I'll be there in a minute. Greg, how are you and the family?" She always asked the same question of the man who drove her family wherever they needed to go, and he always answered the same.

"Doing well, Ms. Stanford, and how are you?"

"Fine." She walked closer to the driver. "Greg, did you get something done about that background check on Victoria?" She made sure Jon was inside the gallery door before speaking.

"He's working on it Ms. Stanford. He said he should have the report finalized later today."

"Mom, you coming?" Jon called from the door.

Meg nodded at her son then looked back at the chauffer. "Call me," was all she said.

"Consider it done." Greg smiled at Meg as she walked in the gallery knowing that she left the job in capable hands.

Inside the gallery, the sound of laughter echoed across the wooden floor as Tom, Alex, and Jon unwrapped the paintings, leaning them against the walls and furniture. Some of the art work held each other up until they found just the right place for each one. There were at least two dozen pieces of original art showing the sea in its many faces, all painted with Meg's bounty from her garden. Organic Art, he called it. The colors seemed to come alive as you stared into the painting, and Meg always found something new in each piece that she hadn't seen before. There were touches of foam as it rolled out from under a wave, a tiny bug that sat on the same pier as the pelican, or the sun glistening off the water from a different angle than she noticed before. But, the raw passion in every painting reflected the man's love of the sea—a love she shared.

"I really like this frame. Mom, what do you think—for my office?"

The modern styled cherry frame pulled the reds from the painting and enhanced them. The frame looked like it was made for the painting—as it was. Alex had commissioned it with the framer before they got there.

"Lovely," Meg replied. "Are you hanging it behind your desk?"

"No, I want it on the other side of the room where I can see it. It's for me, not the general public. Besides, Victoria brought me a new one for behind the desk—an art deco kind of thing that matches the colors of the rug. This is perfect. Alex, wrap it up and tell me what I owe you."

As the men wrapped the painting, Meg stood looking out the door where Greg was on his cell phone leaning against the car waiting on Jon. She was sure he was working on the project she asked him to do.

Then she saw the man with the gray ponytail standing across the street staring at the gallery and not moving. Was she crazy or did he appear to be waiting on her? As she watched, he moved down the street toward the market, and Jon left with his new painting. She must be losing her mind. The man with the ponytail had no interest in her.

Alex and Tom hung the paintings on the walls under the lights and placed several on easels in the middle of the room. Then they climbed the ladder to position the track lights at just the right angle to bring out the best parts of the paintings.

The bell on the shop door rang almost constantly with tourists looking for art as the day warmed up. Some were only there for the air conditioning, but others had been waiting on these paintings for some time. Tom had advertised the one-man art show on his website and with posters around town. Alex was in his heyday. He loved the attention, even though he professed that he didn't. But, who could not be flattered by so many fans at one time?

"I think I'll take a walk around and see what's out there," Meg said after a while. She continued to look across the street at the pottery and was sure there was more where that came from. So many wonderful artists in one place.

"Have you got your cell?" Alex asked around a crowd of onlookers.

"In my purse, yes." Meg slipped from the gallery into the oppressive heat of noon.

The sun on her shoulders, she wandered down Chaparral Street toward the market. The crowds grew denser the further into the market she went. Soon she knew how a sardine felt as it was shoved into a can, shoulder to shoulder with people all looking for the perfect craft, or maybe the perfect restaurant and bar.

A small space in the crowd opened up and she

turned to look into the shadowy alley beside the bar, when her legs were brushed by something hard. She almost fell into a baby stroller with a soundly sleeping toddler, pink from the heat with a bottle sliding out of its still sucking lips. "Sorry," she mumbled, thinking the mother should watch where she pushed her little bundle of joy. The crowd moved on without her.

Suddenly, she was jerked sideways with her arm behind her back and dragged violently down the alleyway. There was a rough hand over her mouth and she smelled the same stale beer breath from earlier.

"No!" she tried to scream, her breath shoved back down her throat. Twisting and kicking, she attempted to get away from arms that were much stronger than hers. Then she sank her teeth into the grimy hand that covered her mouth and held on tightly. This time it was the man with the dirty ponytail that yelled.

"You bitch!" he screamed and slapped her with his other hand, knocking her away and into the brick wall.

Bright spots clouded her vision as her head hit the wall and she swayed, her head swimming. She gritted her teeth and forced herself to not pass out, as she slid down the rough wall on rubbery legs. Landing on top of a loose brick, she gouged her hand on broken glass. She winced as she pulled the brick out from under her hip. Though foggy, she still had the presence of mind to think of a weapon to help even the odds.

The man with the bloody hand lunged at her as she got to her feet. "Help!" she screamed and swung the brick at his head. Blood spurted as he stumbled forward into the brick, making contact.

"Help!" she screamed again, running for the entrance of the alley and the safety of the crowds. She rounded the corner going back the way she came. Elbowing her way through the crowd that probably thought she was crazy, she screamed over and over, "help! I'm being attacked!" She didn't stop until she was again in front of the gallery, and jerked open the door with her still bleeding hand.

"Meg!" Alex shouted over the crowd and ran to her side. Her face was bruised and her vision blurred in the one eye as it swelled. Her hip ached where she fell on the brick that probably saved her life, but she had never felt as safe as she did at that moment, in Alex's arms. She knew he would never leave her. Holding Alex felt like home with all its safety, love, and hope for the future. She was certain about Alex and his feelings for her, and now she was certain of her feelings for him.

"What happened?" Alex led her by the hand to a chair and helped her sit.

"I was attacked. He dragged me off the street into an alley and if it hadn't been for the brick I hit him with, I might be dead now."

"Who?" Tom asked as he helped Alex set her down gently.

"I don't know, but I had seen him before in the crowd and he seemed to be following me. How stupid of me to go out there when I had a feeling about him! But, I thought it was just an accident that he was there every time I turned around. I know now that he was waiting for me."

Alex pulled the cell phone out of his pocket and ran through the contacts for the Corpus Christi police; Detectives Arnold and Samuels. As his phone began to ring, Meg realized she no longer had her purse.

Chapter 30

Victoria pranced around the room in only her panties. It could hardly be called lovemaking, what had just happened in the tiny apartment. The sheets were in a heap on the floor as were his clothes. Hers, she had hung over a chair.

"You know, we're going to have to stop meeting like this. After all, I'm going to be a married woman soon."

"Married woman, yeah, at least for a while," Fitzgerald said, lounging on the bare mattress. "I gave the guy the money to take care of the old lady, and he agreed to half down and half after the job was done. Idiot. He'll never see the second payment. As soon as you're married I'll be on my way to South America to make a new home for us, just waiting on your checks." He sat up in thought. "But, I guess we need to keep him happy until the second deed is done. Maybe we'll have to pay him after all, if we want him to take care of Jon, as well as Meg."

"Yes, I imagine. How much is the second payment?" Victoria said, slipping on her shoes.

"Same as the first, five thousand dollars."

"What? We said five for the whole thing!" She twirled around with her bra in her hands.

"I know, but he was insistent and I didn't know who else to call, so I agreed. I'm sure that another five won't be that hard to get once you're married."

"As long as he gets the job done, and done right." She slipped the dress over her head. "When is he supposed to do it?"

"I don't know. I told him where she was at the festival, then I headed right back here like you said."

"Well, he can't kill her until after the wedding. We're going to the Courthouse on Monday. Tell him he has to wait until after Monday. I don't want Jon in mourning for his mom at the wedding." She paused and turned around. "You're a good boy," she said, leaning down to kiss him. "By the way, did anyone ever tell you that sheets should be washed now and then?"

"Oh, too good for old Fitzgerald's place now, huh?"

"Just wash the sheets before I come back." She picked up her purse and walked out the door.

****

Chung's head hurt where the brick hit him. No, the brick may have been what contacted the soft flesh on the side of his head, but it was the bitch that hit him. Holding on to the wall, he stood up straight and reached into his pocket, pulling out the red bandana. He wiped away the blood and then tied it around his head to cover the gash, his vision still blurry. He felt his way toward the opening of the alley and the crowds on the street.

The families with baby strollers and backpacks paid no attention to him as he stumbled from the alley. Evidently, a drunk wandering out of an alley was not unusual, and the red bandana just looked wet instead of bloody. They would think it was just the heat and humidity that caused it to stick to his head, not a gash from a brick.

Winding through the crowd of onlookers, he wove his way to the Jeep parked a few blocks away. It would take him back to the flea-bag hotel room he had rented, and the bottle that awaited him there.

He needed to think, and that was going to be hard with his headache. He needed a plan to kidnap her and hold her for ransom. He was sure that rich kid of hers would pay whatever he asked to get his mom back. Maybe enough to take care of him for life. But, first he needed a drink. The bitch was going to pay dearly for his throbbing head.

Chapter 31

"So you had never seen this man before?" Detective Arnold asked, for what seemed like the hundredth time.

"Not before today," Meg answered, leaning against Alex with a cold cloth on her head.

"And you don't think anyone saw you dragged into the alley? I mean the crowd was thick."

"I really don't know. There was a hole in the crowd. A large group of people had just passed the alley and I was tripped by a baby stroller. When I regained my footing, I was being pulled into the alley and there was a hand over my mouth to prevent me from calling out. There was so much noise and confusion I doubt anyone would have heard me calling if I had been able. When I did get away, I ran back the way I came, screaming, but no one tried to help. They must have thought I was just some crazy woman."

"Okay, I want you to come down to the station to look at mug shots. Maybe you can pick out a face."

"Not tonight, detective." Alex pulled her closer, protectively. "I'll bring her by tomorrow. I think Meg needs to rest now."

"And I have just the place," Tom said. "I have an apartment over the studio, and there is an extra bedroom. You are welcome to it. I think it will have everything you need."

"You have my cell phone number if you need anything, and we can reach you too. So, gentlemen, if there is nothing else tonight, I think this woman needs some sleep." Alex walked the detectives to the door and closed it behind them as they walked out into the heat.

"No Jon, really, I'm fine. My face is a little swollen, but other than that, I'm fine." Meg sat speaking to Jon on Alex's phone. "Alex and Tom are with me and I'm going to rest. Tom has been generous enough to allow us to spend the night in his apartment over the gallery and you have Alex's number if you need me, since my phone was lost in the scuffle. Thank you, I appreciate it, but I think I'll just stay here for tonight. Maybe we can get together tomorrow. Love you too, Jon." She hung up and handed the phone back to Alex.

"He's a good son." She spoke to the room, but mostly to Alex.

"He gets that from his mom," Alex replied, smiling.

The police said they ran a search for her purse, but it had not been found. It could have become lost anywhere along the way from the alley back to the studio. It wasn't like there was much money in there—she didn't even have a driver's license these days, but she still felt naked without it, and now she had to share a phone with Alex. Independence was something she had always treasured, and she hated leaning on someone else.

Tom opened a bottle of wine and left to pick up some Chinese takeout down the street. Promising to return quickly, he left Alex and Meg to relax. The loft was roomy and comfortable. The small bedrooms surrounded the great room with a kitchen nook off one side. The huge flat screen TV that hung on the wall was on the Weather Channel, which talked non-stop about the hurricane in the Gulf. It was headed for New Orleans, they said, and people there were taking precautions.

The three talked into the night as they ate heaping plates of fried rice, chow mein, and a pu pu platter all washed down with a wonderful chardonnay. Meg was only allowed one glass of wine due to her head injuries, but her water glass was refilled continuously by their host. He was concerned that she might have a concussion even though she insisted she was fine.

Alex changed her cool cloth several times and added ice when it melted. Her face frozen, she finally decided to go to bed as the men watched the weather. Sometime in the night, Alex came to bed too, but she barely noticed. She had nightmares over and over about being chased into alleys. Sometimes Alex would be there to help rescue her. Other times Jon would appear, but most of the time her long lost love, Evan, was calling out to her. "Meg! Over here! Don't go that way, I'm over here!" She woke in a cold sweat with Alex snoring beside her just as the sun was coming up in a turbulent sky, and the wind had changed direction to the northwest. The hurricane was rushing toward Corpus Christi and picking up speed.

Chapter 32

The Weather Channel was on again in the living room when Meg walked out of the bedroom fresh from the shower. She had to wear yesterday's clothes—even had to turn her underwear inside out—but she was clean. Tom had fresh toothbrushes in the bathroom for his guests. It wasn't home, but it was homey.

"The hurricane has changed direction," Tom said to no one in particular. He looked at Alex and then Meg. "Originally, they said it would hit near New Orleans. Now, it looks like Corpus Christi is in its path."

Alex sat on the couch with a cup of coffee in his hands, watching the TV screen intently. He smiled at her with a worried look in his brow.

"You sleep well? Your face is barely swollen. How about some coffee?" He patted the seat beside him.

"I'd love some," Meg replied, sitting down and looking at the television.

"Hurricane Macy, they are calling it. Not a giant one, but headed right for us. Alex, I think those paintings need to go in the basement. I don't see much in the way of crowds today anyway. I suggest we wait a few hours and see if anyone is interested in the festival today or if they are all home making preparations. Then you two can just stay with me until this is over."

"Tom that is very kind of you, but I'm in the same

clothes for the second day and I need to get back home to make preparations too," Meg replied. "Alex, you stay with the paintings and I'll get a ride to the ferry."

"I don't think so!" Alex said, startled. "You're not going back to the island alone, not in this weather."

"Alex, you need to be here for sales and I'll just run back to the island for a few things. It's not my first storm, you know. I can pick some things up for you too, if you need them."

"I don't think that is a good idea; the danger from the storm and then the situation in the alley yesterday? You don't even have a cell phone now. Besides, even if you did, we don't know how long they would be working with this weather knocking out cell towers."

Meg stood and placed her hands on her slender hips. She had spent a lifetime being told what to do. She loved this man in front of her, but he needed to realize she would make her own decisions with or without him. "Alex, I'm going to the island. I'll call Greg to get me to the ferry and you follow later. Besides, he owes me a report this morning. I'm sure he has it ready."

"A report for what?" Alex looked confused.

"I asked him to get an investigator to look into Victoria. He said the report would be finalized today. So, I'll call him and ask for a ride."

"Does Jon know about this?"

"No, of course not. He would never approve."

"Do you think something is up with Victoria?"

"Yes, I do. I did a little investigation of my own and found that my father and her father had business dealings. I have some records of Dad's business before he died. They're in a locker under the bed. I have been looking through them lately since I heard the name Chung. As you know, Graham Stanford was not always a straight shooter. He had business dealings with everyone on the island, and a lot of them were dirty. She keeps moving this wedding up. First it was to be a big event at the country club, and now a quick ceremony at the Courthouse. It doesn't make sense. I want to see the report from Greg and get the paperwork that I left back on the island. I need to put them together and talk to Jon before he makes a big mistake."

"I'll go with you." Alex set down the cup. They could hear Tom on the phone in the kitchen just before he walked into the living room.

"That was our New York buyer. He's in town and wants to come down right now and meet the artist. I told him we had potential weather, but he is insistent. He wants to meet with you and possibly purchase some of the paintings for his gallery. This is a wonderful opportunity. We're going to take you global!"

"Well, I can't stay," Alex said as someone knocked on the door.

"You have to stay." Tom walked to the front door of the gallery.

The handsome limo driver stood in the doorway with a packet in his hands. "Is Ms. Stanford here?"

Meg walked to the door. "Good morning Greg, please come in. Tom, this is our longtime driver and good friend, Greg Thomas. He has been with us for so long we think of him as one of the family."

Tom gestured him in with his hand outstretched. "Nice to meet you, Greg." He walked away, allowing Meg some privacy.

"Coffee?" Meg asked the driver.

"No, thank you, ma'am. I wanted to bring you the report early since we have bad weather coming in."

"Yes, about that, can you drive me to the ferry? I can read this along the way. I need to get back to the island before the storm hits."

Greg looked at Alex. He knew his employer had the last word, but hoped Alex would help him out a little.

"Meg, we talked about this," Alex began.

"And I told you I was going back to the island now so I can get back to safety in plenty of time. Greg will take me to the ferry and I can do the rest myself. We have hours before the hurricane makes landfall. If you want to meet me there later, that's fine. I'll hurry though, so really you can just stay here. Greg, if you will take me to the ferry and then pick me back up in a couple of hours, that would be great. That way you can make preparations with your family for the storm too."

The men looked at each other. They all knew Meg would do what Meg wanted to do. They just needed to make sure she was as safe as possible.

"I don't like it." Alex took his cell phone out of his pocket and handed it to her. "But, if you are going, do it now and take this with you."

Meg smiled and kissed Alex quickly on the lips. "I'll see you in a few hours. You go wow that New York gallery owner." She ran out the door to the waiting limo.

Chapter 33

Mike Fitzgerald paced the small room that overlooked the bay. Having tied up the tug at the dock as best he could, he knew he had to walk away. His livelihood was at the mercy of the ever-looming storm and there was nothing more he could do. That meant he had to rely on Victoria's plan for Jon's money. But, what if Chung didn't accomplish his task? And what if after Victoria, the grieving widow, inherited her millions she forgot about him? He had done his part—would she do hers? He didn't like relying on someone else for his future.

Taking the ferry back to the mainland and leaving the tug to fend for itself really rubbed against the grain. His father would never have walked away—not at least before he started drinking. After the alcohol took over, all bets were off. But, there was a time that his dad would have gone down with the ship trying to get away from the storm. Maybe there was still time. Maybe if he got in the boat and headed south, he could still outrun it. Maybe it was a better bet than trusting Victoria to come through for him.

He reached in the dresser and grabbed a roll of cash—all he had in the world. Then picked up his hat and made a run for the door. He could still catch the ferry if he hurried.

****

The limo parked at the ferry entrance and Greg obediently opened the door for Meg. She climbed out and faced the man who had taken care of her for so many years.

"Ms. Stanford," he began, "Meg, listen to me," he said, grabbing her arm. "There is still time to back out. It is only a few sheets of paper. They are not worth your life. Let me at least come with you."

"No, Greg, go home to your family then pick me up in two hours unless I call you. I have Alex's phone, I'll be fine. I'm just going over and back." She gave him a peck on the cheek before leaving. "Thank you for caring," she called back over her shoulder as she boarded the ferry in the choppy water.

Meg walked to the front of the ferry and sat on the bench away from the cars—not that there were many going out to the island. There would be more coming back the other way.

She didn't notice the man on the other side with his hat pulled down over his eyes who moved away from Meg when she boarded the ferry.

The winds blew the spray in Meg's face and she moved away from the front of the boat as it began its landing sequence. As soon as it was tied up, she was off, walking quickly toward the beach house with the report in her hand and on her mind. She nodded at Poppy as she passed him boarding the ferry, his bag in hand. A bag that probably held everything he owned. His life was so simple, no entanglements, no regrets as far as she knew. He smiled and tipped his hat as she walked past. He saw the man from the dock following her as she left the ferry.

Meg's mind continued to churn thinking about the

report that Greg had given her. She read most of it in the car on the way to the ferry. There were pictures of Victoria Chung and Mike Fitzgerald together in Corpus Christi in what was obviously not just a friendly embrace. Mike Fitzgerald, the son of Evan's fishing partner, was Victoria Chung's lover. Victoria's father was a business rival of her father's, and that meant that her cousin was Robert Chung. He was the man that was suspected of killing Evan. Such a small island for such a large conspiracy! Was there still a conspiracy and was she at the center of it? She knew she was stupid for coming back to the island with the threatening weather. But, she had spent her life protecting the child she and Evan created and she wasn't going to quit now. Jon had to be convinced that Victoria was bad news. She needed those papers.

****

Holding on to his hat in the wind, Fitzgerald watched Meg walking quickly toward the beach house. He ran the opposite way toward the dock and "The Mosquito." He didn't have time to mess with Meg today. Instead, he pulled the cell phone out of his pocket and dialed Chung. "She's at the beach house," was all he said and then pocketed the phone, making a mad dash to the tugboat.

Unlashing the tug, he started her engines. The tank was full of fuel, and there were extra cans on board. He had food and water for a week if he needed it. Checking the instruments, he pulled away from the dock and headed south into the choppy sea and ever-darkening sky. No one was at the dock to see him leave. They all left hours ago, hoping they would still have boats when they returned.

****

Meg rushed into the house and looked around. Her home for the last few years had been the place of the happiest time in her childhood. Here Mariam had taught her to garden and make bread. She had spent hours in the hammock on the front porch when she could get away from her father. When Mariam was home on the weekends, she would knit and hum as Meg rocked back and forth in the sea breeze. It was here that she learned her love of the sea, and here that she felt she belonged. She was like the tiny crabs in the tide pools left behind after the tide went out. She was more comfortable in her tiny beach house than she was in the giant ocean of humanity that was on the mainland. She sighed. Would she ever return to this house? A hurricane had never hit this tiny place head-on like they were warning this time. The house was in bad condition, and it might not take too much to demolish it.

But, she needed to look for the documents in the locker under the bed; there would be time enough for reminiscing later. That was something else Mariam had taught her—your thoughts and memories were your own. No one could take them away from you.

On her knees beside the bed, she pulled the locker out from under the bed and began the search for her father's ledger and receipts. There were Jon's baby pictures and the one picture she still had of Evan. He was never much for having his picture taken, but at least she had one. As she ran her thumb over his face, she thought her memories of him had dimmed. She could not remember his face the way she used to, and the way he touched her when they made love. It broke her heart to think that she could ever forget him, and yet she remembered Mariam's lesson that your thoughts and memories were your own.

There was a backpack in the closet that had been Jon's when he was a child. She wondered why she had kept it, until now. Opening the door of the closet, she reached for the light and realized just how dark it was getting in the middle of the day. The clouds were rolling in at a much faster rate than she had expected and then the winds changed direction again. With a clap of thunder, the lights went out in the bungalow.

Chapter 34

"I really like these and want to take them with me today." The man in the loafers without socks stepped back from the painting again.

"Well then, let's wrap them up," Tom said.

"And maybe this one too," he said slowly, rubbing his chin and taking off his tortoise shell glasses.

"Listen." Alex was getting antsy. "There is a hurricane in the gulf and it is headed our way. If you want these paintings, let's load them and you need to be heading north. This weather is not going to wait on any of us."

The rail-thin man in the seersucker suit looked irritated and breathed deeply, letting it out slowly. "Okay, if you insist," he grumbled. "But maybe that one too."

"Let's do it!" Alex almost shouted. "I have to get back to the island to get Meg. Tom, can you do the honors? I've got to go."

"Of course, and I'll take the rest of them to the basement."

"Mr. Blair, it was a pleasure and I'm sure we'll see each other again, hopefully under better conditions. Tom will help you pack up, and I suggest you head north in that rented car and not look back until you reach safety," Alex ran for the van and pointed it toward the ferry.

Screeching to a stop at the ferry parking lot, he got into the short line going back to the island.

"Last trip, Mack!" called the tugboat captain, gesturing. "This is the last trip out and we won't wait long to return. So if you're sure you want to go, you'd better hurry."

The planks rattled as Alex drove onto the almost empty ferry. The crew directed him to his spot to make the ferry as balanced as possible. Alex put on the emergency brake, wondering how much good it would do if the boat capsized in the storm. As the sky darkened, the wind whipped the waves into a wild frenzy. The man with the gray pony tail backed up behind the wall and remained out of sight. Only crazy people would go back to the island now—back into the mouth of the lion. And they were some of the crazy ones.

The time it took to get to the island seemed to double, pushing against the ever increasing wind. The salt spray covered everyone and everything on the ferry as they pushed forward. Alex used his windshield wipers several times so he could see out.

Finally, arriving at the island Alex drove off the ferry quickly. He stepped out of the vehicle and stood looking at the dock for Meg. His plan was to grab her and head back as soon as the tugboat captain said they could leave. But, the dock was deserted. No one was left on the island—or the ones still there were not going back. He raced toward town and his shop. Maybe she would be there and ready to go. If not, he would keep going to the house.

He stopped the van and ran to the shop, calling her name. The door was still locked so he knew she hadn't been there. He would check the harbor before he went to the beach house. Maybe she was saying goodbye to her neighbors. Now that she was aware she had friends, she would hate to leave them. But, surely they were already gone.

The van's tires squealed to a stop at the dock where the fishing boats were tied up. Waves crashed into the dock, threatening to pull it loose from its moorings. Boats collided with each other and waves sprayed up over the office building creaking in the wind. The air smelled of ozone. Meg was nowhere to be found. When he agreed to let her go back to the house for a few things, he was afraid they would be too late. The woman was so stubborn and set in her ways. Where was she?

Chapter 35

Tom was climbing the steps from the basement one last time when he heard someone banging on his front door. He put the plywood he kept for hurricanes on his windows, and he had all the paintings from his gallery safe and sound. At first he thought the noise was the wind until he realized the knocking was rhythmic. That was not the wind; someone was outside in the weather trying to get in.

With the windows covered, he had to open the door to see who was there. There swaying in the wind, stood Jon.

"Is Meg here?" he called loudly over the storm.

Tom opened the door wider. "Come in, Jon. No, your mother and Alex went back to the island. They should be back soon. You want to wait here for her?"

"You let her go back to the island? There's a hurricane out here!"

"She was insistent. Besides, the Weather Channel said we had hours before it hit land. Obviously, it moved in faster than we thought. But, I'm sure they'll be back soon."

"Well, when she does come back, don't let her leave this time! I'll be back." Jon ran back to the limo. "Get this thing to the dock where the ferry comes in—and hurry!" he yelled at Greg.

Greg slammed on the brakes at the dock and Jon

was out of the car before it stopped. He ran to the dock to greet the ferry on its way back in. It made much better time on the way in than it did on the way out, with the winds blowing it toward the mainland.

Standing facing the water, Jon could barely stand up. The wind was getting stronger and it was starting to rain. When the tugboat captain brought the ferry into the dock, Jon scanned the cars onboard. Damn! Alex's van wasn't there and neither was his mother.

"Where is she!" he yelled at no one.

Watching the people step off the ferry, he realized how few people came back from the island this trip. He recognized Poppy as he walked Jon's way.

"She got off on the island. And that Fitzgerald guy was right behind her," was all he said.

"You saw her? Did you talk to her to find out what she was doing?"

"No, she just nodded at me when she got off was all." The bum and his small bag of possessions walked away to wherever he went when he was not on the island.

Victoria climbed out of the back seat smoothing her skirt and walked up behind Jon, putting her arms around him.

"She'll be fine, honey. She probably just decided to stay on the island. You know how crazy she is about that house. They say the storm won't be that bad," she said, rubbing his shoulders. He turned in a rage.

Jon thought of the beautiful dark-haired woman at the country club smiling warmly at everyone she met, calling them by name as she made her way to where he sat at the table. Victoria really knew how to work a crowd. That was one of the things he loved about her—

her ability to be at home wherever she was. When they played tennis at the club, her short, white tennis skirt showed off the tanned legs. She had zeroed in on Jon the first time she saw him, walking his way smiling. Yes, she knew how to work a crowd. And probably him.

"That is my mother you're talking about! I have to get to her. Greg! Get me the Coast Guard and Victoria, call a cab home. I'll be here until I can find her."

Taken back, Victoria stood with the wind whipping her long black hair in her face. She looked at her fiancé a moment and then, like the little girl that lived on the island years ago, stomped her foot and turned around, pushing against the wind as she huffed back to the office at the dock. Her cell phone to her ear with her hand cupped around it, she called for a taxi. Maybe Jon and his money weren't worth it after all.

Chapter 36

Looking out into the lagoon, Alex slowly realized that the tiny lights in the distance were going away, and probably not coming back. The last ferry had left early without them, and Meg was nowhere to be found. Could he have missed her and was she on the ferry?

He raced back to the van and drove to the beach house against the wind and rain. There were no lights on in the house. Was she still there, or did Jon find a way to get his mother off the island?

Screeching to a halt, he pushed the door open against the ever increasing wind, climbed out of the van and began the arduous trek to the house on the beach. He had to check to make sure she was not still there. If he didn't find her at home, he didn't know where else to search.

The garden groaned and creaked as plants and trellises whipped back and forth in the wind. This side of the island faced the open ocean and the tiny house would get the brunt of the storm. Limbs lay everywhere and he climbed over broken plants to the backdoor of the house. Pulling it open, he shouted her name. Was she home?

"Meg! Are you still here?" Alex called, running into the kitchen.

"Alex?" she came around the corner with a backpack and flashlight in her hands. "You came back for me!"

"What took you so long? Why didn't you make the last ferry?"

"Why didn't you? Why are you here?"

"For you! And the ferry has already left. I think we may be the last two people on the island. I was hoping maybe Jon found a way to get to you and you wouldn't still be here."

"I know I was being silly, but I was looking for some of my father's papers. I have to help Jon and they might not be here when I come back."

The windows rattled until Meg was sure they would break. The huge gust of wind that blew the screens on the porch in, suddenly stopped and sucked them back out. Then the rattle became a groan, which became louder. And the ripping began. Ancient nails being torn from their rotting wood creaked as they were pulled against their will, holding on to nothing—flying up and over the top of the house. Within an instant, the porch walls and roof were gone and the floor was about to follow.

"Time to go!" Alex shouted and shouldered the backpack full of Meg's mementos.

Meg ran back and grabbed the painting off the wall.

"Leave it! You'll never be able to hang on to it. Stay close with your head down. We just have to reach the van and we should be relatively safe." He grabbed her hand and pulled her from her precious home, but she hung on to the painting, tucking it under her arm.

They ran out the back door, not even trying to shut it behind them, and clawed their way through the garden, Meg never letting go of Alex's hand and the precious painting under her arm. Without him, Meg was sure she would have been swept away in the wind. A tomato cage with the plant still inside flew past her face, so close the leaves brushed her skin. She thought she would be impaled on its pointed wire feet. Then the painting was savagely ripped from under her arm and flew into the dark sky after the wire cage. She gasped, or maybe the breath was sucked out of her, it was hard to tell.

"I'll paint you another one, come on!" Alex's voice was barely heard over the storm.

Once at the back of the garden they began the climb up the sand dunes, holding on to grass along the way. At the top they stopped, crouching to see what might be blowing their way before standing. From the top of the dune, Meg could see there were no lights left on in the harbor. Either they had been blown out or everyone had already left.

Climbing over the rise, suddenly the rain increased, wrapping around them like soggy bed sheets on a clothesline, entangling them in their own wet clothing. Meg could see the van parked off the side of the road in the distance. It rocked in the gusts like it might take off flying at a moment's notice. Heads down and stumbling into the wind they pushed forward together against Mother Nature's fury—one step forward and sometimes two or three back. Once they reached the asphalt, they found it slick and Meg fell on her knees. They made little headway until they got back on the soggy sand.

Alex pulled the door to the van open and shoved her inside. Climbing to her side of the vehicle she realized he was still outside struggling to pull the door shut against the relentless wind. Meg crawled back to his side and the two strained together to pull the door closed. Finally shut, she found she was in a wet heap in his lap as he started the engine. She dragged herself to the passenger's side of the van, and she looked out the windshield as he backed up and saw the angry black sea crashing more and more closely into the defenseless beach house she called her home.

The windshield wipers could not keep up with the driving rain as they drove slowly against the wind, the van rocking from side to side. It was less than half a mile into town—a distance she had walked daily for years, her wagon in tow, but it seemed to take hours to get there. Dodging limbs in the road, debris blew past and sometimes crashed into them. Meg knew they would have never survived without the safety of the steel surrounding them.

Finally, she could see the tiny town—but no lights were burning. The lines must be down already. She wondered who was left on the island after the final ferry left. Almost reaching the shop where Alex lived and worked, they were stopped by a huge tree lying across the road.

"We're going to have to hoof it from here," Alex said, opening the door and pulling her out behind him. She tried to close the door against the wind, but it was fruitless. "Just leave it open," Alex said as he dragged her to the shop where the glass from the window and door were already blown out.

Once inside, Meg felt safer. She could at least stand up, even though the wind still howled outside.

"To the back. There's a door behind the closet that leads to the basement. I don't think it leaks, at least I've never seen water any time I've been down there." Alex led her to the back of the shop.

Opening the dark closet Meg felt her way through the clothes, pulling them out and throwing them on the floor. She clamored to the back and reached for the doorknob. Suddenly a light shone behind her. "I was hoping this flashlight still worked," Alex said steps behind her.

The moldy basement walls felt wet and rough as she slid her hands along them, creeping down the ancient wooden steps—knowing she could fall through at any moment. It might be dark and moist, but it was better than outside where the winds howled and the devastation was ripping the town apart.

Alex shone the flashlight at the bottom of the steps. In the corner under the stairs were stacks of boxes, canning jars, and a bench. Alex moved the jars onto the floor and set the backpack beside them. Then he directed Meg to the bench, wrapping her in a heavy woolen coat that smelled of moth balls.

"I grabbed the first thing I could find in the closet on the way down." He stood in front of her wearing an all-weather overcoat over his sodden clothes. Grimy blankets lay in the corner covering things she didn't want to think about, but Alex picked one up and shook the dirt loose. He brought the dirty blanket to the bench and pushed it up against the load bearing wall under the beam. "We can at least sit on it to make things more comfortable," he said, spreading it on the bench.

Sitting in the dank basement, Meg's thoughts turned to her tiny house and the garden behind. It would all be destroyed—maybe completely gone. Where would she go and what would she do? The last place she wanted to return to was Corpus Christi. But, first they had to survive the night and thanks to Alex, she might.

The shop groaned ominously as if it was alive. She looked up. Upstairs doors banged open and glass broke in the back of the shop. Then the heavy footsteps began. Someone was in the tiny shop. Maybe someone had come back to save them! Meg was on her feet in an instant. "Jon!" she started to yell when Alex grabbed her arm.

"Shhh," Alex said with his finger to his lips. "We don't know who that is. It could be someone needing shelter or who knows. As far as we know, we were the last ones on the island," he whispered. "After the incident in the alley, we can't be too careful."

Alex doused the light as the footsteps rounded the corner to the closet. Clothes strewn about would show the way to anyone who was looking for them—good or bad.

The wind gusted and the shop groaned urgently, and then the first foot touched the top of the stairs. The hair on the back of Meg's neck stood up and she was suddenly shivering in the damp, musty wool coat. She moved closer to Alex, but he leaned away, reaching for the box of canning jars. He sat back up with two jars in his hand and handed one to her. They watched the steps for life and heard the creaking as the intruder neared the bottom of the steps.

"Anyone home?" called a gruff voice.

Meg knew that voice. It belonged to the man in the alley that had tried to kill her. And her shivering became more violent.

"That's the guy from the alley," she whispered.

Alex held tightly to the glass jar with one hand and

the flashlight in the other. He was prepared to use the only weapon he had to protect himself and Meg.

The flashlight in the man's hand suddenly clicked to life and swept the room. Alex and Meg leaned back against the wall, trying not to be seen. Something shiny and large was hanging from the intruders hand as he walked into the basement room.

The light arced around the room once more, and this time landed on Meg and Alex huddled against the wall.

"Well, look here. It's the heiress and her boyfriend," he said in a slurred voice. His head still wrapped in a bloody red bandana, he looked around the room. He knew he had the upper hand in this fight.

"Stay away from us," Alex said more forcefully than he felt. His hands were still by his sides to hide the glass jars.

"Well, I'm not going to hurt you, Meg. I want you alive. The boyfriend, though, has to go." He stepped into the middle of the tiny room and Alex clicked his flashlight on in the intruder's eyes. Automatically, he reached to shade his eyes. The huge meat hook dangled from his hand. The silver hook was used to move sides of beef in a packing house. If it could move half of a cow, it could do some real damage to a live human being.

Standing quickly while the intruder was still blinded, Alex rushed at the man and smashed the jar into the side of his head. Staggering, he swung the hook at Alex. Alex jumped back at the last possible moment before the sharp point caught him in the mid-section. Meg screamed from the other side of the room.

Chung swung the hook again and Alex caught it

with the flashlight, trying to yank it out of his hand. But, the artist was no match for the murderer who had more experience with the violent hook. The flashlight went rolling to the other side of the room. Meg instinctively dove for the light. Grabbing it, she rolled onto her back and shined it into Robert Chung's eyes again. That was all the time Alex needed to back away and reach for another weapon. The only other things in the basement were more canning jars and blankets. Grabbing what he could find, he smashed the end of the jar against the moldy wall and held the jagged glass in one hand, and the end of a blanket in the other. Maybe he could ward off the blow of the hook with the snapping blanket.

Chung smiled a greasy smile. "Like shooting fish in a barrel." He swung the meat hook one more time at Alex. Alex whipped the blanket at the intruder and caught the meat hook, but not before it tore through his shirt and sliced the skin underneath. Warm liquid oozed under his clothing. Alex swung the jar, grazing the man's face. Chung backed away, wiping his face with the back of his hand in astonishment.

"Okay, no more playing." He lunged toward Alex again. Holding one end, Alex lashed out with the blanket to throw the murderer off balance, and this time Chung caught it, pulling him in closer so he could plunge the hook into Alex, when something hard hit his hand. Meg flung the flashlight from the other side of the tiny room, knocking the hook from Chung's hand. Both men dove for the hook just as a horrible ripping began above them. All heads looked up to see the ceiling bulge up and then come crashing down with horrible finality.

The hurricane was demolishing the shop, trapping all who were inside. The last thing Meg remembered was the sound of the crashing ceiling and being unable to move her legs. Then everything went black.

Chapter 37

"I don't care if there's a storm out there! My mother is on that island and you have to get me out there to find her!" Jon yelled into the phone. Greg managed to get through to the Coast Guard—no small feat considering the weather. But, their job was search and rescue and Jon expected them to do it. He was used to telling people what to do, and he was used to his subordinates following his orders. Things weren't working out so well this time.

"I want to talk to your boss. What was your name again Sargent? Well, Sgt. Warner, who is your supervisor? Get him on the phone. What do you mean, he's busy?"

"Sir, maybe I could help," Greg said, taking the phone from Jon's hand and patting him on the shoulder. Jon stood helpless, a feeling he was not used to. He was always in charge. This time things were different. Tears sprang to his eyes as he looked out into the angry ocean from the office at the dock. The windows rattled and the waves crashed up against the hurricane proof structure. Would he ever see his mother again, and why didn't he insist she stay with him last night? At least he could have kept her from going back to the island.

"The good thing is that it's a fast-moving storm," Greg said, handing the phone back to his employer.

"Why is that a good thing?" Jon asked, beaten.

"The eye of the storm is directly over the island right now and will be headed for us next. They expect the storm to turn south and follow the coastline. When that happens the choppers will be ready to go. The search and rescue units will be sent to the island and I've secured a seat for both of us to go with them. I'm sorry I couldn't talk her out if it, Sir. I love her too. I'll not sit idly by to see if she is found. I'll be in the middle of it with you."

Jon relaxed. Greg was right. He did love Meg too, and he was going to risk life and limb to help find her.

"What about your family?"

"Safe at home in the basement. Besides, if the storm is moving back out onto water like they think, it will all be over with soon here on the mainland."

"You're a good man, Greg. Remind me to give you a raise."

"I don't need a raise, Sir, I just need your mother back."

Chapter 38

"The Mosquito" headed south along the shoreline. If the weather caught up with him, Fitzgerald didn't want to be out in the middle of the ocean. He needed to be close to shore in case the boat was swamped.

The engine roared, coughed once—and then sat silent.

"Not now," Fitzgerald said to no one. He was alone and now was not the time for the aging engine to die. "Shit!" he said, jumping down the few steps to the engine room. Smoke billowed from the motor and he slid the tool box out from under the cabinet.

Running back topside, he dropped the anchor. Repairs might take a while and he didn't want to be dragged out to sea with the sky darkening behind him. Then he descended the steps again, hoping he could fix whatever was wrong this time. He had been the mechanic and captain of this bucket of bolts for a long time and they had a special relationship. She broke down, and he fixed her back up.

He thought about the radio but knew his "Mayday" would go unheard with the storm. The radio waves would be full of emergency calls. Besides, he didn't think he wanted to run into the authorities right now. He and Victoria had been living on the edge lately and they were close to being set for life. Well, she was. He hoped she still remembered his name after she became a Stanford.

He sat on the floor and folded his knees under him where he could reach the toolbox.

"Okay old girl, what's wrong this time?" he asked as the wind began to howl. The stormy sea wasn't going to make this repair job any easier as he and the tool box rocked from side to side. Out to sea alone with a hurricane coming at him in a hurry, Fitzgerald knew he might be making the last repair of his life on his tugboat.

****

Meg woke once or twice in the hot, twisted basement. Her legs felt paralyzed and she tried again and again to sit up, to no avail. Even slight movements were impossible. Each time she did, the pain through her right side was excruciating. She was pinned under the collapsed building and no one knew where she was. Then she thought of Alex.

"Alex!" she tried to shout. But, it came out in small exhales, making it harder to breath. She thought she heard movement from the other side of the room before she passed out again.

As she lay in the rubble, she dreamed of her beach house and the tide pools. Tiny fish swam around her legs and crabs walked sideways to get away from her. The ocean waves roared as the tide threatened to come back and swallow up her minute world, but she would stay until the first wave tried to take it away. Then she saw Evan down the beach walking toward her. He smiled at her and extended his hand. She looked into the deeply tanned face and emerald green eyes that danced when he smiled. Was this real? Her love. How long it had been since she had seen him. How long since he had wrapped his arms around her, and then he stopped before she could reach out and touch him.

"Time to go, Meg," he said, stepping back. "Time for you to go back."

The wave rolled into the tide pool and sucked out the first of the tiny fish. She knew the next wave would be bigger. She looked out at the insistent sea and saw it coming for her—the next wave was much larger than normal.

"Go back," he said and then he disappeared as she reached for him.

"I think I've found something!" shouted a voice above her head over the roar of the heavy machinery. She thought the storm was still raging, then she realized that the noise she heard was the sound of a crane sliding down and scooping up debris in its massive jaws. "Hold it!" the voice shouted. It sounded oddly familiar.

Wood and bricks were pulled from over her head. She heard the sound of voices calling out to each other and shouts of "stop!" at the crane operator. Suddenly, there was movement all around her and the board directly above her head was pushed aside. Heavenly sunshine poured down on her head. The air smelled sweet, like after a rain. A gentle hand brushed her hair back from her face. "Mom," said a familiar voice and then she passed out again.

Meg woke to excruciating pain as the boards that held her legs captive were moved and she was lifted out of the basement. Something warm and wet ran down her shirt and her breathing remained painful and shallow. She might never breathe deeply again. Looking up, she saw Greg's smiling face as he helped Jon and the Coast Guard captain move her onto a stretcher. A needle was inserted in her arm, but she barely felt it.

She looked around, but Alex was nowhere to be seen. "Alex?" she asked, but she was told not to talk. "Where is he?"

"I told you paperwork wasn't worth your life," Greg said, pushing her hair back away from her face.

"Backpack," she whispered and passed out again as the pain edged away.

Chapter 39

"There is someone I think you will want to talk to," Jon said to the Corpus Christi detectives after leaving his mother's side at the hospital that day. Meg remained in a drug-induced coma to aid her healing, but the doctors assured Jon she was going to be fine. "His name is Poppy, and I'm sure he knows more than most anyone around. He came to me after the ferry brought him to the mainland the night of the hurricane and told me that Mom went back to the island, and she was being followed."

"It's too late for the ferry tonight, but we can get one of the police boats to take us over. Will he be there?" Detective Arnold asked.

"Where would he go? He lives there in an apartment and I can show you where. He knows everything that goes on at the island. Let's go." Jon quickly rose from the chair.

As the police cruiser pulled up to the dock where the ferry sat at night, Jon helped tie it off and climbed out of the boat. He directed the detectives down the road toward the less desirable side of town. The tourists never traveled to this section of the island. The streets were dark with a few lights still shining through some of the windows. Most of the island was asleep.

Jon walked up old wooden steps that led to the upstairs apartment. The light was on at the top and the wooden door open, but the screen closed. With no air conditioner, the windows were open too, and the sea breeze blew through the rusty window screens.

"He's there," Jon said, knocking on the door and calling out Poppy's name. "You in there? It's Jon Stanford." The lights were on, but there was no movement inside the tiny apartment.

Jon knocked again.

"You guys need something?" came a call from down below. Poppy stood at the bottom of the stairs with a fishing pole over his shoulder and a tackle box in his hand.

"I thought you were home with all the lights on."

"Works, don't it?" the old man said as he climbed the steps past the police detectives and worked his way to the door.

"What works?"

"You thought I was home. I leave the lights on so no one will rob me. If they think I'm home, they'll just keep on walking."

"Who would rob you on this island?" Jon asked.

"Well, there are new people on the island all summer long, and you just never know," he said as he opened his door and ushered them inside. "Jon, you've never been to my place before. I'll bet you're here to talk about Meg. Am I right?"

"You're right, sir," Detective Samuels said.

"It's just Poppy, not sir."

"Okay. Can we come in and talk to you?"

"Sure, but there ain't a lot of room."

The square room had yellow peeling wallpaper and a bed along one wall that doubled as a sofa. The kitchen area held a small table with two chairs. The sink was full of dirty dishes that were probably never washed. A tiny two-burner stove held a pot of leftovers from his last meal, and the rusty refrigerator hummed noisily through a door that didn't close completely. The only other room seemed to be the bathroom that backed up to the kitchen. Jon wondered if the apartment was up to code, but he knew it was the best that the old man could afford. Without it, he would be sleeping on the dock.

They were gestured to the chairs and Jon took one turning it around and sat. Poppy plopped down on the bed. The detectives stood with their hands behind their backs except when they pulled out notebooks and began to write.

"What do you know about Mike Fitzgerald?" The detective wrote in his notebook as Poppy began to speak.

"Well, I know he weren't a nice guy, if you know what I mean. He paid me a hundred dollars to find out where Robert Chung was these days. I mean that's a month's rent so I took it. I asked around, found out that he hadn't gone too far. He was just over in Rockport. Didn't take me long to make that hundred dollars."

"How did you find him?" Jon asked.

"I knows people, you know. When you been around as long as I have, you get to know people. I don't have a lot to do, so I took the ferry to Corpus and asked around. I found him quick. He'd been there all along. He didn't run far."

"All along? Since when?" Detective Arnold looked quizzically at the old man.

"Since he was hired to kill Evan and then told to leave the island."

"Evan Miller?"

"Yeah, Miller, that was his last name. You know, Jon, your daddy. I guess this ain't the first time you heard that story, right?"

"No," Jon said, thinking of his mother. "It's not the first time I've heard that my father was murdered. But, why did it take you until now to mention it to someone?"

"Nobody asked me, I guess. Anyway, I didn't have nuthin' to do with it only carry the package from Graham to Robert. I had nuthin' more to do with it than that. If I'd known what the note said, I'd never have delivered it. I like your mom. She's always been good to me. I didn't know until afterward what the note and the money was for. I ran errands for Graham all the time. Probably 'cause he knew I couldn't read the notes. Well, that and he paid me to keep quiet. So, I did."

"You delivered the note to Robert Chung telling him to murder Evan Miller, and that note came from Graham Stanford?" Detective Samuels' question sounded more like a statement. "How do you know if you couldn't read the note?"

"Well, I heard Graham talking to one of the guys that worked for him about it. He said he had me deliver the note 'cause he knew I wouldn't talk. I guess it's okay to talk about it now that Graham is dead. I don't work for him no more."

"Yes, it's okay." Jon ran his hands through his hair. His mother was right. Robert Chung had killed his father and then thirty years later he was hired again. Had Fitzgerald hired Chung to kill his mother too—or kidnap her? Anyone who knew them knew that Jon would pay anything to keep his mother alive.

Kidnapping her was a better money-maker than whatever Fitzgerald had paid him to kill her. And did Victoria fit into this story?

"Do you know Victoria Chung?" Jon looked the old man in the eye.

"You mean your girlfriend?" he looked at Jon quizzically.

"Is there anything you don't know?"

"Not much I guess, at least not on this little island. I know most everyone and they probably know me."

"I imagine you're right. But, what do you know about Victoria?"

"Well, she's your girlfriend. You probably know all about her." Poppy squirmed uncomfortably on the bed/couch. "What you might not know is that she grew up here on the island. Her daddy was a shipper until he went broke. Little Vicky Chung hung around the dock all the time as a kid, and then as soon as school was over she took off to the big city and never looked back. I don't think she liked it here very much."

"So, she and Robert were related?"

"Sure. Her dad and his dad was brothers. Robert was always the bad guy in town. If there was trouble, he was in the middle of it to be sure. So when Graham needed some dirty deed done he paid Robert. It always made Vicky's daddy mad that Graham helped him along in his life of crime. That much was sure. They had words over it more than once."

"So, Mike Fitzgerald paid you to deliver a note to Chung to either kill or kidnap Meg, is that right?" Detective Samuels asked.

"I ain't in any trouble am I?" Poppy looked pleadingly at Jon.

"No, I'll see to it you don't get into trouble. Just tell the detectives the truth. It's important."

"I was paid a hundred dollars to find Robert Chung and deliver the note to him just like the first time. But, really I didn't know the note was about Meg. I would have never done that to her. She's a nice lady. Is she gonna be okay after the building fell on her?"

"Yes, she will be okay, and I'll tell her you asked about her. It will make her feel better."

"By the way," the detective began, "do you know where Mike Fitzgerald is at this time?"

"At the bottom of the ocean? I don't know for sure, but the last time I saw him he was heading for the dock and his tug's gone. I guess he got on it and headed out in the storm."

"Okay, that's all for now. If we need to talk to you again, we know where to find you," the detective said.

"Well, if I ain't here, I'll probably be down on the dock. I live there as much as I do here."

"Thanks for your help." Jon handed him the cash that was in his pocket. He was sure he needed it, and informants were used to being paid. As they left the shack, walking back down the wooden stairs, Jon made a mental note to include the apartment in the renovations they had planned for the island. He at least needed a place to sleep that wasn't a firetrap.

"Well, I think we need to pick up Victoria Chung and find out for sure where Mike Fitzgerald is," Detective Arnold said once they were back on the boat. "If you give us the address, Mr. Stanford, we'll take it from here. No need to wait until morning."

"I could do that, but I think I want to be there when you pick her up. I want to see the look on her face."

The detective shrugged as the boat flew across the water of the lagoon that was smooth as glass, toward the lights of Corpus Christi.

****

Jon smiled as he rang the doorbell in the middle of the night at Victoria's apartment. He rang it three short times in succession so she would know who was at the door. The bedroom light came on, and a shadow could be seen as she grabbed her robe and walked to the front door. Then he leaned on the bell until she opened the door.

"What the hell is wrong with you," she began and then she saw the detectives. Jon stood in front of the door with a sneer on his face and his hands in his pockets.

'Hey, Vicky!" He knew she hated being called that.

"Have you been drinking?" Victoria pulled her robe together.

"Not a drop—yet. These are my good friends Detectives Arnold and Samuels and they want to talk to you about Robert Chung."

She jumped slightly and then smiled. "Well, Jon, honey, let me at least get some clothes on if I'm having company."

"Sure, honey, I'll go with you." Jon pushed in the door past Victoria with the police in tow.

"Ms. Chung, we need for you to come to the station with us for some questioning. Mr. Stanford can go with you to get dressed."

At the police station Detective Arnold told Victoria that Mike Fitzgerald had rolled on her and said she was the brains behind the whole operation. He said she had hired her cousin Robert to kidnap and eventually kill

Meg. He also said Fitzgerald was in the next room giving details of their affair, and that she had put up the money so she could get her hooks into Jon and his fortune. It didn't take long for Victoria to talk, saying that it wasn't her idea but Fitzgerald's. He was, after all, the one who had tried to blackmail Meg, and when that didn't work he hired someone to kidnap her. She also said he was jealous of Jon so had decided to kill Meg to get back at him. The lies went on into the night until eventually Jon became tired of hearing them and went home. His mother had almost lost her life trying to protect his. He would spend the rest of his life trying to repay her.

****

Meg dreamed a thousand dreams as she lay in the hospital bed—some of Evan, some of Jon as a baby, some of her father in his office at the dock, and many of Alex. When she awoke a few days later surrounded by the constant beeping of machines and bright lights in her face, she had no idea where she was.

Jon lay sleeping in the recliner by her bedside with the tattered backpack in his lap. Her son that she loved so much was by her side. How long had it been since the accident she wondered, and where was Alex? Trying to sit, she felt for the button on the side of the bed, but her right arm wouldn't move. It was tethered to the bed with an IV poking out. Wiggling her toes, she was certain everything was still there. She rolled onto her left side to feel for the button she knew should help her sit up. Pain seared through her body. It was the same pain she felt in the basement. But, determined to sit, she felt again for the button and found it this time. The foot of the bed began to rise. It was the wrong button. Feeling up along the bedside, she found another and pushed. This time her head started up.

"Augh!" She yelled when the pain went through her again and Jon woke with a start.

"Mom! You're awake. We were beginning to wonder about you. Are you in pain?"

"Bed. Up too far," she managed to squeak out.

Jon rounded the bed in a step and pushed the button to lower her head. "You've had some injuries. But, the doctor says you'll be fine. You punctured a lung, but you will heal. You could have been crushed."

"Alex?" she asked, fearing the worst.

"Right here." Meg could see just his head as Greg pushed him in the wheelchair through the door. He was smiling, and his longish gray/brown hair was disheveled. There was a bulge under his hospital gown from a bandage, but he appeared healthy under the circumstances.

"Alex." She attempted to say his name again, reaching for him. But, it barely came out as a breath.

"Alex saved your life." Jon moved aside so the wheelchair could be moved closer to Meg's bed. "We found him on top of the other guy who had a meat hook sticking out of his chest. It's miraculous that you are both alive. I have Alex here to thank for saving my mother."

Alex moved closer and took Meg's hand in his.

"And I have my mother to thank for saving us both from Victoria. I read the report and saw the paperwork you went back to get. The police also talked to Poppy who knows everyone, and he had seen Victoria and Fitzgerald together. He also told them about Graham having Evan killed. He was sent to deliver the message about the plans because he couldn't read the note from Graham. I guess Grandpa Graham knew he couldn't read. He's known all along about Dad's murder, but no one asked him before. You risked your life for me," Jon said with tears in his eyes. "And don't you ever do it again."

"You're worth it," she squeaked then smiled at Alex. He leaned over to kiss her and grimaced at the pain. She pushed the button to lift her head again no matter how much it hurt, and met him halfway. The kiss, though painful for both, was the sweetest they had shared in the few months they had been together.

"Victoria?" Meg asked, looking at her son.

"She has been charged with two counts of solicitation of attempted murder. When the detectives told her that Fitzgerald rolled over on her, she spilled the beans. No one's seen Fitzgerald, actually. His boat is missing and the authorities think he may have made a run for it in the hurricane. He is either in Mexico or dead. We don't know for sure."

Meg smiled. Neither of them would bother her family again.

"Okay, this is sweet, but I have to check on my patient." A short blonde nurse with a stethoscope around her neck pushed through the crowd with a clipboard in her hands. She adjusted the IV for Meg's drip and laid her bed back down. When she smiled, her brown eyes danced. "What a great family," she said when the exam was over. "You're healing nicely, Meg, and with this support group, you will do well."

Meg talked for a few minutes, but found she couldn't keep her eyes open. Her family and friends left her to sleep, then Jon sat down in a chair with a thump as Greg took Alex back to his room to rest.

"You look like you could use some coffee," said the blonde nurse. "We have some in the nurse's station, even if it is terrible."

"I'd love some coffee. Is there somewhere to eat around here?"

"The hospital cafeteria, but it's as bad as the coffee. However, there is a little bistro across the street that has great sandwiches and coffee to die for."

"Do you get a break?" Jon asked.

"In about thirty minutes," she responded with a smile.

"I'll meet you here in thirty minutes and we can get something to eat if you would like?" Jon smiled.

"I'll be back." She walked away with her clipboard.

Jon rubbed the stubble on his chin as he watched the nurse walk away. He couldn't remember if he had a shower this morning or if that was yesterday. He had been living at the hospital. But, one way or another, he didn't have time to go home and clean up. There was, however, a shaving kit in a bag in Mom's room that he could take advantage of, if he could do it quietly without waking her. He didn't want to look like a derelict in front of this woman. After all, he was single again.

Chapter 40

Sitting in the sun on the balcony at Jon's high-rise apartment, Meg relaxed. Alex was coming to get her. He would pick her up and take her back to Sandhill Island today. He had been staying with Tom in the loft above the gallery and visiting when he could. The painting was keeping him busy, but he called every day now that she had a new phone.

The bandage on her side was smaller with each visit to the doctor and the wound was healing nicely. Her favorite boutique delivered clothes of every variety. They hung around her bedroom waiting for her to decide which ones to keep and which ones to send back. They were of every variety and color, but none that she could wear to weed her precious garden.

The doorbell rang and Meg rose to answer it with only a small twinge in her side—something she was getting used to. When she opened the door, there stood the second love of her life. Alex had sunflowers in his hand and a smile on his face. He said nothing, but leaned in to kiss her squarely on the lips. He tasted like quiet nights on the beach and a long life lived in peace and tranquility. He tasted like love, and he tasted like her future. She smiled back.

"Did you buy those from some crazy garden lady on the street?" she asked.

"I haven't seen any crazy garden ladies. But, I did

get them off the street from a vendor, does that count? They reminded me of you sitting in the sunshine. You're in your element with the sunshine bouncing off your hair." He ran his hand through her hair and pulled her to him, kissing her again, more deeply this time.

She placed her hand on his stomach and felt the bandage there; the cut on his torso that probably saved her life. He would have died for her. The man with the meat hook that followed them to the shop that day planned to kill him and kidnap her. Money did such strange things to people. She would have given him all she had if he had just promised to go away and never come back to bother her or her family again. But, he assumed he had to kill for it.

Evidently, her father felt the same way. The rumors were probably true that he had Evan killed so his daughter, the heiress, wouldn't marry a fisherman. At least, Poppy was saying that it was true. He had known for years, but no one ever asked him.

Was Graham sorry when he found out Meg was pregnant with Evan's baby? Jon was very much like his grandfather in many respects, but he had his father's traits too. Traits like caring for his mother and those loyal to him.

Meg overheard Jon sending Greg and his family on a cruise to thank him for helping to find Meg. Not that you could buy that kind of loyalty. Greg would have done it with no payment. But, he earned it and it was a lovely gesture on Jon's part. It showed his soft side that many did not see.

She reached for the flowers and carried them in to the kitchen with one hand, holding Alex's hand in her other. A blue/gray contemporary styled vase that

Victoria had probably picked out sat on the bar. Meg filled it with water and placed the home-grown flowers in it. She was sure Victoria would not have approved.

"Are we going to Jon's office?" she asked.

"Whenever you're ready."

"Well, let's go. Then you promised me a trip to the island."

Sitting around the boardroom table, coffee was served from a silver service. Jon's assistant, Joan, passed the paperwork to her boss then handed him a pen.

"These deeds transfer title to the original owners of the land on Sandhill Island." Jon signed the bottom as president of the corporation and then handed them to Meg to sign as secretary. Meg had no idea there would be so many at first. She and Jon had pored over her father's books for nights on end to see who had been cheated on the island where she had grown up. Meg's hand cramped after a while, and all she had to do was sign her name. After Joan notarized the stack, each document would be filed with the county and then given to the respective owners. Meg was insistent that the land be returned to the original owners and Jon agreed with her, even though he wanted to make sure no one decided to sue over the deals.

The backpack Meg risked her life for held the paperwork showing the deeds that her father had retained after he drove his neighbors near bankruptcy. And now they would get the land back into the hands of the rightful owner.

"This next document grants the right to the named party to dredge the harbor at Sandhill Island so that it is available to all who have need of its waters and sets up a perpetual corporation to keep said harbor safe in a manner that is available to anyone who has need of it," Jon said in a lawyerly manner and signed the bottom of the document, handing it to his mother for her signature. Meg signed with a flourish and smiled. She and her son had vindicated her family. She felt she could see Evan on the other side of the room with that same smile on his face that she loved. He would have been proud of her today—her and their son. He had grown into a good mix of the two of them, and had the tenacity and head for business of his grandfather. He was honest and loving, but no one would ever run over him. Meg could not have been more proud in that moment of her son, or the corporation they had created with her father's funds.

"Let's take these to the island and see if maybe Sam will fix us dinner," she said to her two favorite men in the world.

"I doubt it will be fit to eat," Alex said. "He has been having to truck in vegetables. But, we can find out."

Chapter 41

They took Alex's rented car to the ferry and once more to the island. The waves blew a salty spray in Meg's face as she stood beside the car. Breathing deeply, the sea air reminded Meg of all that she had been missing while she recuperated in Corpus Christi. Meg and Alex watched as the tugboat pilot maneuvered them closer to the newly repaired dock. A private company, with money to spare, had anonymously repaired the dock so the ferry was able to make its treks to the mainland and back again.

The tiny town had begun their cleanup. The people of Sandhill Island were used to the many faces of the sea and sometimes cleaning up after her tantrums. The plywood that had been screwed into the window facings saved most of the glass. Even though some paint was needed, most emergency repairs had been made.

The shop that Alex rented and the vegetable stand were gone and the cleanup was finished. The landscape was bare ground missing the buildings. The basement had been filled in and smoothed over, waiting for sea grass to grow in the sandy soil.

The heavy-set man in the white chef tunic was watering his new herb garden behind the restaurant. His top button undone, he glanced up as Alex parked the car in the parking lot.

"We're not open until dinner," Sam Taylor said

and then a smile spread across his broad face. "Meg! And Alex, how are you? We've missed you both so much!" He trotted toward the car, sweating in the sun.

He opened Meg's door and hugged her tightly, not waiting for her to exit the car, then ran around to shake hands with Alex. The back door opened and Jon's long legs stepped out. "And Jon, what a surprise."

"Good to see you, Sam," Jon said, holding out his hand to the chef. "When is dinner?"

"Anytime you want it. No fresh vegetables, but I can come up with something palatable." He turned back to look at Meg and Alex. "I can't get over how great you look. I guess you are healing nicely? We were all so worried."

"I'm fine, really. We both are. I wouldn't be alive though if it hadn't been for Alex." Meg stood next to Alex holding his hand. "We don't want to put you out, Sam, but we were hoping to have a town meeting here tonight. We'll pay for dinner, but could you organize something? We would like to talk to our neighbors," Meg said.

Sam looked confused. "Sure. Everything okay?" Meg nodded. "Okay, I'll pass the word. How is six o'clock?" He paused. "You mean everyone?"

"Everyone who can come. We have an announcement." She smiled at Sam who seemed to relax.

"Let's drive down to the beach and see what's left of it. I haven't been down there since the storm. And I want to see the harbor too. Sam, we'll be back around six and anything is great for dinner. We really appreciate you taking care of this for us."

"Well, Meg, there isn't a lot to see, but let's go."

Alex opened the door for her to sit. The three back in the car, they waved goodbye to Sam and drove to the beach, and what was left of the house.

Meg's heart caught in her throat as she walked down the sandy hill and surveyed the damage. Heaps of wood lay strewn up and down the beach as she stepped gingerly between them, careful not to step on a nail. Where the house had been, lay part of the floor and she dared not walk across it even though she wanted to. She wanted to be in her bedroom one more time, or the front porch that she loved in the evening with the rocking chairs that were no more. But, she knew it wasn't safe.

Instead, she walked around the back to her once-lovely garden and surveyed the damage. Most of the plants were gone and some were just broken over and dead from neglect. She looked up the hill at the sand dune she climbed the night of the hurricane and shivered at the memories of tomato cages flying past her face.

"It's all gone," she sighed.

"But, we're alive to see it," Alex said, hugging her lightly. "And we can rebuild if you like. The gallery wants me in New York next week and sales of the paintings are going through the roof. I don't think I'll need the help of the Stanford Corporation anymore. I am an artist—and no longer a starving one."

"There are new and better ways of building that are hurricane proof," Jon said. "I was surprised a thirty mile an hour gust hadn't taken that little shack down. I worried about you all the time living here. A major hurricane could still take out any structure on a beach, but a new one, built to hurricane codes, would stand up fairly well."

"Do you really think we could?"

"Yes," they both replied at the same time.

"And maybe we could have a wedding there too," Alex said with a sly smile. Meg looked at his face as he looked out to sea and then back at her. He got down on one knee and held her hand.

"Meg, will you marry me? A starving artist?"

Jon cleared his throat, "Excuse me, I'll be over there." He walked away and looked out to the ocean.

"You're not a starving artist."

"No, so would the heiress marry a successful artist? One who is only successful because of her?"

"I didn't make you successful."

"You're avoiding the question," he said.

Meg smiled, and in the middle of the debris that used to be her life she said yes to a new one. He kissed her lightly at first, then more deeply holding her head in his hands. She wrapped her arms around the man she loved kissing him back—in the garden where the relationship started.

Still in a state of shock from the proposal, Meg insisted they drive to the dock before the meeting. All that was left were pilings standing in places where the dock had separated. Some of the debris had been pushed up on the shore, others were entirely gone. The office where her father's place of business once stood and the first place she had talked to Mike Fitzgerald was missing—blown away and then pulled out to sea. More of her old life was gone, but not all of that life had been good. The only boats tied up at the dock were Paul's shrimper and a tugboat she didn't recognize. But, it could be rebuilt.

At dinner that night Sam put out the spread that

earned him a reputation as a first class chef. Everything was fresh. He was growing a small herb garden behind the restaurant with the help of a new employee, a gardener from the mainland. He was again trucking in produce since Meg's garden had blown away. But, the fresh herbs gave things a new flair.

Meg walked around the restaurant talking to all the people from the island that she had known for so long. It was good to be home even if she really didn't have a home to go back to.

After most everyone had eaten and drank their fill, Jon stood and tapped his glass with his fork. "The reason for this meeting tonight is to talk to the good people of Sandhill Island. As you know it has made my family what it is today." There were some quiet groans in the crowd. "But, with that in mind, my mother has insisted—and I agree with her—that we repay you and hope to make amends for any wrong doing that may, or may not, have been done to you in the past."

Meg stifled a grin at her son who would always be a lawyer.

"So with that in mind, we have prepared deeds conveying all property back to the rightful owners who may have been wrongfully, or without careful consideration, taken from them." The murmurs began at the back and then slowly grew louder.

"Sam," Jon said, handing a document to the chef that prepared the evening meal, "this deed, properly filed at the county, conveys your parcel of land here on Sandhill Island back to you and your family with the apologies of the Stanford Corporation. If there are any questions, please feel free to call my office." He handed the file-stamped deed and a business card to Sam and then began to hand out the other deeds to the people in the crowd. "You are all land owners again, and the rent due the Stanford Corporation will not be due this month or any other in the future."

The room sat in stricken silence, then Sam began to clap and soon every hand in the crowd joined in. Stunned faces began to smile as they read over the deeds that were handed out and the conversations started as they compared deeds. They were land owners!

Meg smiled warmly at her son, knowing they had done the right thing.

"Sam, is there still an empty apartment over the restaurant and would you be willing to rent it to Alex and me?" Meg asked after the meeting was over.

Sam stopped in his tracks. "Rent it to you?"

"You own the place. We might need it for a year until the new house is built. You know how slowly these things go sometimes. We'd be happy to sign a lease if you like. It might take a year to get the building finished and we'd be happy to pay you well for it. I think it might be a short tourist season this year with the clean-up and such. Alex and I have decided to rebuild in the same place as the original beach house."

"No, Meg, I won't rent to you. That apartment is not much anyway. But, you can live there for free. I owe you so much, and that little place is just sitting there empty."

"No, Sam, we insist on paying you rent. You could rent it out to tourists. We just don't want to live in Corpus until the house is built. Alex will be going back and forth to the gallery a lot anyway, and I could be close to my garden. I hope to get it back up and in shape before long."

"I don't know what to say. Of course you can stay in the apartment, but I really don't feel right taking money from you."

"Well, if you don't rent to us, someone else could use it. So, if you will agree, we'll get some furniture delivered. Please say yes."

"You know I can never turn you down, Meg." Sam smiled. "Of course you can use the apartment; that way I'll get the vegetables sooner rather than later."

****

"The one place in the world that I love almost as much as Sandhill Island is Italy," Meg told the architect. "I think I want an Italian villa, but built to make it as hurricane proof as possible."

"That can be done. We'll sink the anchoring piers deep into the sand to begin with. I have a plan in mind that I have never used, but it could be modified to make it hurricane proof."

"Alex and I will be back and forth to Corpus Christi while he goes to the gallery that has his paintings, and here is my cell number. We live in an apartment on the island, but you can find us whenever you need us. I like to stay home as much as possible to work in my garden."

"I'm sure I can find you, Ms. Stanford, and will call you soon with the results of my design."

The day the builders came to begin work on the new home, the townspeople came out to see the bulldozers and equipment

"Meg," Sam said, standing as he helped her with the perennial plants that were returning. "I think these guys are here to see you."

She stood and shaded her eyes with her hands, watching the trucks of building supplies stopped at the top of the sand dunes. Her dream home built in a familiar place was about to become a reality.

Epilogue

The string quartet warmed up in the screened-in gazebo that sat in the middle of the garden beside a fountain. The sea breeze blew lightly past the rose bushes growing beside the house. The Tuscan style home extended out the back where the patio made a second outdoor living room and turned the corner to the art studio off the other side of the house.

Sam ran in circles, making sure the buffet was perfect. The shrimp on ice in the kitchen would be brought out at the last minute. The wedding cake sat on the table next to the champagne fountain, surrounded by rose petals.

The bride in an ivory lace tea-length sun dress with matching sequined sandals walked out the front door and leaned against the pillar that held up the roof. She looked out at the water as she fingered her bouquet of sunflowers and sea oats hung with ivory ribbons. The waves crashed far out in the ocean and then rolled in gently onto the shore that was their front yard.

Kicking off her shoes, she walked barefoot to the tide pool that gathered at the edge of the water and dipped one toe, careful not to soil the dress. She looked longingly out at her beloved ocean and thought she saw a fishing vessel, and then blinked. It was gone. Down the shore, a deeply tanned man walked toward her, smiling.

"He loves you, Meg." His bright emerald eyes crinkled at the corners in the sun.

"I love him, too." She smiled. "But, I'll always love you, Evan. We didn't have enough time."

"We had enough. We created Jon, and that was enough."

"He's wonderful," she said.

"Thanks to his mother."

"Meg?" Alex called from the porch. "You coming?"

"In a minute," she said, twisting around to look at her groom. When she turned back, Evan had disappeared just like the fishing boat she thought she had seen. She smiled and walked back to the new house, digging her toes in the sand as she went.

Inside the living room, the minister stood next to the fireplace. Jon and the nurse that took care of Meg while she was in the hospital were hand in hand. She was short, blonde, and kind. Everything that Victoria wasn't. They made a nice couple. Meg hoped she would stay in the family and they would become good friends.

The entire population of the Island was in attendance. Greg, the driver, and his family, Tom from the gallery, the women from Meg's favorite boutique on the mainland, and the employees of the salon were also invited to the smallest wedding of the year. This time, they brought the spa and boutique to her. They spent most of the morning getting Meg ready for her big day while drinking mimosas. Even the fishermen and tugboat crew from the ferry were in attendance, and they insisted that Poppy come, too. After all, he was part of the community. The wedding at the new hurricane-proof home they had been building for a year was filled with their closest friends.

Later, Meg hardly remembered the minister's words, but she remembered when Alex kissed her. She was where she was meant to be—at home in her new beach house with the man she loved and the friends she made along the way. Finally, she would have the life she had always wanted, but was afraid to try. She could be more than just a mother—she could be a lover, wife, neighbor, friend, and philanthropist. What more could you expect of one life?

After the short ceremony, everyone traveled to the back of the house and the simple garden filled with tables and chairs among the plants. With their arms linked, Alex and Meg drank a toast to their new life together, and their friends cheered loudly.

Sam served everyone his finest fare of shrimp, pasta, bread, and fresh vegetables—many from the new garden in Meg's backyard. The cake was big enough for twice the number of guests and was decorated in red raspberries, strawberries, and blackberries with sprigs of mint and lavender.

Sitting in the shade of umbrellas, Meg and her new husband ate dinner and wedding cake into the evening with their friends. The sunset reflected off Meg's glass of chardonnay as she held it up to the decreasing sunlight, watching the colors as they spread across the liquid. And there, by the squash, she saw him. The little brown bunny munched happily along with the other guests at Meg's new home; a symbol of her new life.

A word about the author...

Peggy Chambers calls Enid, Oklahoma home. She has been writing for several years and is a twice-published author, always working on another.

She spends her days working in an office and her nights and weekends making up stories. She has two children, five grandchildren, and lives with her husband and dog.

She attended Phillips University, the University of Central Oklahoma, and is a graduate of the University of Oklahoma. She is a member of the Oklahoma Writers' Federation, Inc., Enid Writers' Club, and Oklahoma Women Bloggers.

There is always another story weaving itself around in her brain trying to come out. There aren't enough hours in the day!

~*~

Ms. Chambers writes a weekly blog at
http://peggylchambers.wordpress.com/
Please "like" her on Facebook at
https://www.facebook.com/BraWars
or connect with her on Twitter at
@ChambersPeggy

Thank you for purchasing
this publication of The Wild Rose Press, Inc.

If you enjoyed the story, we would appreciate your
letting others know by leaving a review.

For other wonderful stories,
please visit our on-line bookstore at
www.thewildrosepress.com.

For questions or more information
contact us at
info@thewildrosepress.com.

The Wild Rose Press, Inc.
www.thewildrosepress.com

Stay current with The Wild Rose Press, Inc.

Like us on Facebook

https://www.facebook.com/TheWildRosePress

And Follow us on Twitter
https://twitter.com/WildRosePress